ABOUT THE AUTHOR

Cathryn Hein is a best-selling author of rural romance and romantic adventure novels, a Romance Writers of Australia Romantic Book of the Year finalist with *Santa and the Saddler*, and a regular Australian Romance Reader Awards finalist.

A South Australian country girl by birth, Cathryn loves nothing more than a rugged rural hero who's as good with his heart as he is with his hands, which is probably why she writes them! Her romances are warm and emotional, and feature themes that don't flinch from the tougher side of life but are often happily tempered by the antics of naughty animals. Her aim is to make you smile, sigh, and perhaps sniffle a little, but most of all feel wonderful.

Cathryn lives in Newcastle, Australia, with her partner of many years, Jim. When she's not writing, she plays golf (ineptly), cooks (well), and in football season barracks (rowdily) for her beloved Sydney Swans AFL team.

To discover more about Cathryn and her books, visit cathrynhein.com

ALSO BY CATHRYN HEIN

Rural Romance

Eddie and the Show Queen

Elsa's Stand

The Country Girl

Chrissy and the Burroughs Boy

Wayward Heart

Santa and the Saddler

April's Rainbow

Summer and the Groomsman

The Falls

Rocking Horse Hill

Heartland

Heart of the Valley

The Horseman's Promise

Romantic Adventure

The French Prize

Scarlett and the MODEL MAN

CATHRYN HEIN

First published 2020

ISBN 9780648582021

Copyright © Cathryn Hein, 2020

All rights reserved. Except in the case of brief quotations embedded in reviews, no part of this publication may be reproduced, transmitted or distributed in any form or by any means, including photocopying, recording, or other electronic or mechanical methods, without the prior written permission of the copyright holder.

Scarlett and the Model Man is a work of fiction. All names, people, places, businesses, events or incidences, are fictitious and a product of the author's imagination. Any similarities to actual people, living or dead, or actual places or events are entirely coincidental.

Cover Art by Kellie Dennis at Book Cover by Design
www.bookcoverbydesign.co.uk

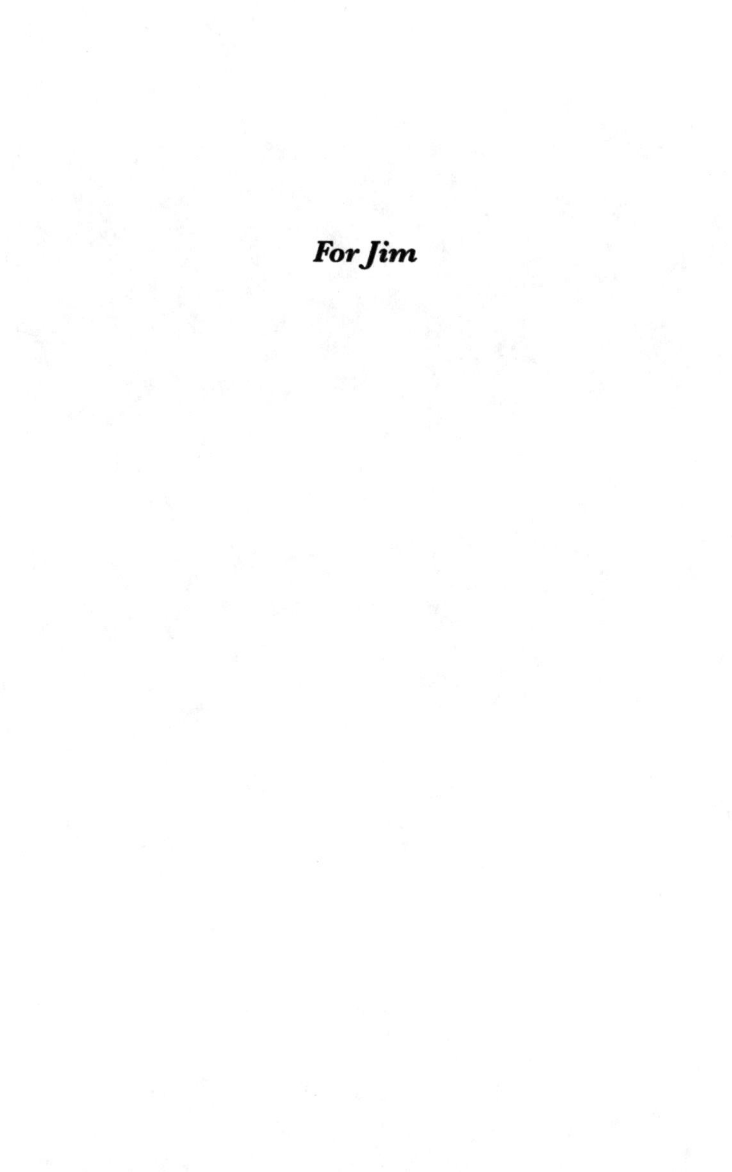

For Jim

ONE

IT WAS *Crowns* that started it. Scarlett had been fine until that painting. More than fine. On the biggest creative high of her career. Then she'd agreed to a charity commission and *poof!* A month after the artwork went up for auction, her muse evaporated like a wish-drained genie.

It wasn't *Crowns'* fault—as cutesy as it was, the painting was still accomplished and she was proud that its sale had raised thousands of dollars for local causes. It was her. Something had changed inside. Scarlett wished she knew what.

She stared at her current effort then at her palette knife. A glob of blood-red polymer paint glazed the blade's end, making it appear more butcher's equipment than up-and-coming artist's. She smiled wryly at the thought. The only thing being butchered around here was her art. As for up and coming, right now Scarlett was more down and out.

Her gaze lifted again to the ugly thing she'd created, which was so lacking in life, despite the vibrant colours and thick layers of paint. Scarlett's usual technique was delicate brushstrokes, sometimes fine felt pen, occasionally pencil or charcoal, and in rare moments dried flowers and plants or other natural media. Her work was complex and elaborate, almost labyrinthine as it wound around the shapes, mysteries and power of womanhood. One critic had called it 'phantasmal', like a drug-addled dream. The sort of work you could regard for hours and still not discover all its secrets.

The canvas in front of her had none of that. It was, to put it mildly, an abomination. The change in technique had led nowhere except to prove she hadn't solved her problem. Perhaps she never would. The creativity that had lit up her mind and fed her talent since university, which had weathered passion and pain and a hundred distractions in between, was dead and showing no sign of a Lazarus-like resurrection. Not even a twitch. And its timing couldn't be worse.

Oh, the absolute shittiness of it. The. Absolute. Utter. Complete. Shitty-bitty-arsedness of it.

With a howl, Scarlett stabbed the palette knife into the canvas and yanked down, the resulting tear ripping a scream of its own. She stabbed again and again, imitating the violin screeches from the shower scene in Alfred Hitchcock's *Psycho* with each blow.

On a roll, she began to dance like a boxer, lunging in for a gash, twirling to backhand a puncture, her screeches morphing into mad giggles. She bumped her worktable. The water in her brush jar sloshed dangerously. Paint tubes tumbled to the floor. Manic, she stomped on one. A geyser of red shot up her bare leg and hemmed her shorts with glossy colour.

'Come on,' she said, skipping sideways and gesturing at her bad art. 'Fight me.'

But the canvas, and her muse, remained mute.

She kept up the macabre dance. The *Psycho* screeches morphed to an out-of-tune version of Metallica's 'Enter Sandman' as she sent her work off to never-never land. The canvas was large—a two-hundred-centimetre square of quality cotton she'd stretched and gessoed herself. Scarlett's usual canvases tended to be half that size, but she'd gone big in the hope that the increased scale would fire something inside the black-hole deadness of her creativity.

It had fired something all right. A kind of mad violence that was far too enjoyable to be healthy. Yet knowing that didn't stop her frenzy, even when she'd reduced the canvas to shreds. She wanted to kill whatever was wrong with her, raze it until it was nothing, too. Create a void for her muse to flow back into. Besides, destroying bad art was surprising fun. Perhaps it might even prove cathartic.

As she charged for one last stab, a loud bang pounded the old dairy's southern window. Scarlett yelped and whirled, the palette knife dropping from her hand and striking the top of her boot, where it left a red gob on her steel-capped toe.

A shadowy head bobbed against the dusty glass. Then a pair of hands cupped the window and a distorted face was thrust between them.

'You right there?' yelled Jed. 'Hang on, I'm coming in.' Next breath, her neighbour had flung open the screen door and was rushing towards her, chased by a small swarm of pesky flies. He skidded to a stop, his eyes bulging and his walnut face paling. 'Flippin' heck.' Jed peeled off his t-shirt, balled it up and stretched out one arm, as though pacifying a frightened animal. 'Steady there, Scarlett love. I'm here now. Just tell me where you're hurt.'

Scarlett's heart was thrashing like a drowning swimmer. Her lungs taut from fright and hungry for air, she spread her fingers across her chest to ease the ache. Taking that as a sign, Jed thrust his t-shirt over her hand and pressed hard.

'It'll be okay, love. I'm here. We'll sort it, get you help. Just hold steady.'

She gulped in a breath. 'No.'

'Now, now, just you stay calm. Here,' he picked up her loose hand, 'you hold that tight while I call an ambulance. Where's your phone?'

'I don't need an ambulance.'

'It's all right, love. I know you're frightened and lost a lot of blood—' He glanced down and blanched. 'Holy Mary mother of Joseph.'

'Jed!'

He jerked at her yell, his crinkled jowls wobbling.

'I'm fine. It's paint.' She kicked at the spent tube of quinacridone crimson.

'But I heard screaming.'

She gently pushed him away, shook off his t-shirt and held it out for him to put on. 'It wasn't screaming.'

'Not screaming?'

'Maybe a little bit of screaming.' The smile she gave him was more of a sheepish wince. 'I was having a moment.'

He regarded her with disbelief, then gave a little shake of his head and removed his gaze from hers to take in the room. The kitchenette and small lounge-dining area of the converted dairy were in their usual neat state, but her studio space looked as if a werewolf had gone mad in it.

The heavy drop sheet Scarlett had spread to protect the timber floorboards was streaked with red, the fallen palette knife lying in a large stain like a discarded murder weapon. Tongues of torn canvas drooped over the easel shelf as though panting at the bloody floor. Tubes of polymer paint littered the surrounds, most, thankfully, with their lids secure. The fountain of crimson was waste enough.

As for the flies Jed had let in, the majority had dived straight for the sticky paint and were buzzing hysterically as they tried to extricate their bogged feet.

Scarlett cringed. Admittedly, she wasn't the tidiest of artists, but this was a new low even for her. 'I'll clean up, I promise.'

Jed dismissed that with a flick of his hand, his gaze still on the mess. He said nothing for a moment, lips pursing and unpursing as if working their way up to speech. 'Is this some sort of modern art thing?'

'No.' Scarlett sighed. 'Just frustration.'

'Right.' He nodded, still clutching his t-shirt. 'Right. I'd ... um ...' He paused to give the palette knife a worried glance. 'I'd better get back to the girls.' He lifted his shirt. 'Sorry.'

'Don't be.' She touched his arm. Jed was a nice man and she hated frightening him. He was also her landlord. With her lease now month to month, Jed and Faye could have her out with thirty days' notice and then where would she be? The apartment wasn't perfect—far from it with its sweatbox interior, irritating flies and unique poo smell—but it was cheap and came furnished, and she couldn't afford the distraction of a move, not with her muse AWOL and her London residency only three months away. 'Thanks for checking up on me.'

'Sure. No problem.' He pulled his shirt over his head, straightened it over his grey-haired chest and slight pot belly, and eyed the canvas again. 'You sure you're all right? Faye's home, if you want to ...' He gave an awkward shrug. 'You know. Do the woman thing.'

Scarlett smiled. 'Thanks, but I'll be fine. And I need to clean up.'

'Right you are, then.' He headed for the door, paused for a moment to look back at her, then nodded and disappeared. From the open door came the sound of his dairy herd as they plodded their way down the lane to the milking shed.

Scarlett sighed and plucked up the paint tube. Its once fat belly was caved in, its essence almost depleted. Heat prickled her eyes and her nose got that horrible leaky feeling that foreshadowed tears. She swallowed them down. Scarlett had never been the sort who cried over spilled paint or anything else for that matter, and she wasn't about to start now. Whatever was wrong with her she had to battle, not sob over.

Besides, tears attracted flies, and she hated those little bastards.

When the studio was returned to relative order and the flies began dropping like, well, flies, thanks to a dose of chemical warfare, she made herself a cup of tea, donned a floppy fabric hat and headed outside. Unlike the past week, when yet another stinking summer heatwave had frazzled her temper further and made walking outside like entering a furnace, the day was mild. The air was redolent with the distinctive aroma of silage and cow dung, and mellow with the moos and grumbles of Jed's herd as the first cows filtered back into the lane after milking. Beneath the radiant sun, their black-and-white coats shone like glazed porcelain.

Scarlett leaned an elbow on a rail and sipped her tea. Normally, she found the herd comforting. She loved their big, curious eyes, the pale pink of their broad nose tips, the slow roll of their bony hips and the sway of their huge udders. They seemed free of cares, and if they did have any, they'd swat them aside with a swish of their long tails.

Even their calm, slow-moving progress didn't ease Scarlett's mind. It was early February, and her London residency began in April. It was an extraordinary opportunity to create, learn, attend exhibitions and other events, and most importantly make contacts in the international arts community, all while living rent-free in a community environment and with utilities covered thanks to the Australian Government. Only four residencies were granted each year and competition for places was high. To be chosen was an enormous honour and a sign of faith in her talent.

Talent that had now deserted her.

Tears threatened again. Scarlett made a mewling noise as pain and unfairness threatened to overwhelm her. How was she meant to take up her residency if she couldn't paint? She'd be a fraud, squandering not only taxpayers' money, but faith—her own and that of those who'd believed in her.

Swallowing the burn in her throat, she studied the landscape, hunting for answers. Apart from the sprawling metal irrigation rigs and the occasional house, windmill or stand of shelterbelt trees, the view to the south was flat and featureless. Even in this rich, lower south-eastern corner of South Australia, where the seasons were milder than the rest of the state, the harsh summer sun had beaten the unirrigated paddocks to wheaten yellow and made the grey of exposed ancient limestone reefs appear silvery. She'd had several goes at painting it, but it gave no joy. Landscapes had never been her thing. People were. Women especially.

Her feminine series had been hugely successful, with collectors agitating for more, but the urge to produce those complex works had disappeared with *Crowns*. Now months had passed and Scarlett was still empty of inspiration. When she tried to force it, all she produced were passionless, colourful messes like that of this morning. Works as barren as she felt inside.

She caught movement in the distance. Jed's grandson, David, heading out on a quad bike. He was a gorgeous-looking boy of eighteen, overloaded with hormones, confidence and the thrill of a life that stretched wonderfully ahead. As a twenty-nine-year-old, Scarlett hadn't known whether to be flattered or appalled when he'd made clear his interest. She'd laughed and fobbed him off, a rejection he'd fortunately accepted with good humour.

She watched him ride, admiring the inverted triangle of his silhouette and the cute man bun his grandfather loathed but which Scarlett imagined many local teenage girls dreamed of untying. If she were younger and not so jaded, she'd probably dream the same.

David alighted to inspect something near the laneway gate, then stood with his hands on his hips, head swivelling slowly as he surveyed the farm. His gaze found Scarlett and he waved. She waved back, smiling. He really was an attractive lad. Perhaps she could paint him one day, capture that burgeoning energy. The way he seemed balanced on the precipice of adulthood, potential stretching ahead. His life's direction unknown but calling like an adventure.

The thought ruffled something inside her. Wingbeats of excitement, reminiscent of the flutters she used to feel when she had an idea for her feminine series.

Breath suspended, she stared at David as he remounted, but her mind wasn't on him. Her mind was on that fluttery idea. On youth versus maturity. On potential versus true power and strength. Potency. And not that of the feminine.

She'd captured that multiple times already, perhaps to the point of boredom.

Masculinity, on the other hand ...

A grin formed. Scarlett knew what she needed now: a man, but not just any man. She needed a model man.

And she needed him now.

TWO

'I CAN'T FIND HIM,' said Scarlett. 'I know he must be around here somewhere, but ...' She puffed out her cheeks and released the breath in a *pfff* sound.

She was dining with Audrey Wallace at Restaurant Ten, Levenham's most upmarket eatery. Scarlett would have preferred a pub meal. She wasn't a starving artist, but she couldn't be profligate, either. If this creative drought continued, she'd run out of works to sell and have to dig into her Felix settlement account, money she'd earmarked for emergencies only. Not just that, she needed savings for London. It was an expensive city. Even with her accommodation and utilities covered by the residency grant, she still had to eat and buy art supplies.

Fortunately, today Audrey was paying.

'What about your sittings with Jedidiah?' the octogenarian asked in her distinctive Queen Elizabeth II voice. The gold rope necklace and sapphire pendant around her throat made her appear nearly as rich.

Scarlett shook her head.

'I take it Faye objects?'

'No, I don't think she minds. It's me. He just doesn't do it for me.'

It had been almost two weeks since her masculine epiphany, and in that time Scarlett had paced half the streets of Levenham in search of the perfect model. She'd wandered through car dealerships, mechanics' workshops, agricultural suppliers. Scanned supermarkets and clothes stores. Eyed bankers and accountants and postal workers. She'd faked inquiries for plumbers, cabinet-makers and every other trade she could think of, attended a basketball game and cricket match, and even a chess match at the local library. All without success.

Levenham wasn't a big town—around fifteen thousand inhabitants—but it was a major service centre for the district's agricultural, forestry and fisheries industries. Young men and women from surrounding smaller towns and farms tended to gravitate there for employment, if they weren't heading to university, jobs elsewhere or overseas adventures.

A man shortage wasn't the problem. The problem was finding the right man, preferably one who wasn't attached. This was a conservative community, after all. A husband or boyfriend life-modelling for another woman, no matter how professional, wouldn't go down well. Nudity tended to have that effect.

In desperation, Scarlett had asked Jed to sit for her and he'd been kind enough to oblige, although dressed in his dairy-farming best of faded shorts and t-shirt. It had helped a little and she'd made some promising preliminary sketches, but the story she wanted to tell wasn't that of a man in his early seventies, no matter how fit. Scarlett wanted a man in his prime, whose potency was at its peak.

And she wanted him in all his glory, which was not something she could ask of Jed.

'Doesn't make your juices flow. I can't say I'm remotely surprised.' Audrey nudged her. 'He doesn't do it for me, either.'

'I should hope not. He's far too old for you.'

'Quite,' said Audrey, who was notorious for her appreciation of attractive young men.

They returned their concentration to their beautifully prepared meals. Scarlett's locally caught velvet crab with roast cherry tomatoes and prawn oil had been so precisely decorated with micro herbs she'd wanted to photograph it. Knowing Audrey would disapprove, she'd refrained, though she'd taken her time before eating to memorise the design and colour combination. Audrey had declared her King George whiting with pipis in prosecco-butter sauce sublime, which was high praise from a woman many considered the town's matriarch. And proxy lady mayoress, if the rumours about Audrey's long affair with mayor Barry McClintoff were to be believed.

'My grandson-in-law would fit your brief.'

'He would. Absolutely.' Sleepy-eyed Josh Sinclair was a gorgeous timber craftsman in his thirties. He was also married with a baby. Scarlett hadn't had much to do with his beautiful wife, Emily, but had enough experience to know she could be as haughty as her grandmother when the mood took her. 'I'm sure Em would have no problem at all with Josh nuding up for me in the name of art.'

'No,' said Audrey on a sigh. 'She's like her mother in that way.'

'Nothing like you, of course.'

Audrey chuckled, then broke into a cough. Scarlett frowned. That cough sounded unpleasantly phlegmy, which was hardly surprising given Audrey's cigar habit, but Jed had mentioned a summer flu strain that was doing the rounds. No matter how invincible she considered herself, Audrey was in her eighties and vulnerable. She was also a friend, albeit an irascible and occasionally demanding one.

The older lady caught her look and narrowed her blue eyes. 'Don't you look at me like that.'

'You should stop smoking.'

'And you should stop being judgemental.' Audrey took a long sip of riesling and eyed Scarlett. Glaucoma in her left eye had distorted her pupil and made it appear partially collapsed. To many her stare was disconcerting, but Scarlett merely wondered if it hurt. Even if it did, Audrey was unlikely to admit to it. She was a strong woman, and Scarlett had delighted in capturing that essence on canvas, back when her creativity was alive and thriving. 'You should be worrying about yourself rather than me.'

'Believe me, I am.'

'I'd offer my grandson, Digby, but Jasmine—his girlfriend, although I do wish they would hurry up and announce their engagement; this faffing about has gone on long enough, in my opinion—would be even more disapproving than Emily.'

'Too pretty, anyway,' said Scarlett, setting her chin on her fist. 'I need someone good-looking without being pretty. Rough but not ragged. A perfectly imperfect man, like ...' She tried to think of an actor who'd match her criteria and instead caught sight of a man the size of a small country walking past the restaurant's floor-to-ceiling windows. She pointed her fork in his direction. 'He'd do.'

Audrey swivelled to look, then laughed. 'He would indeed, but I'm afraid you'll run into the same problem there. That's Harold Argyle.'

Scarlett gave her a blank look.

'It was his brother, Edmond, who nearly defeated Alice Lindner to win the Wine Show crown.'

At the mention of Alice, Scarlett's scalp prickled. She had nothing against the girl—in fact, she'd immediately warmed to the pixie-like blonde when they'd met—but it was Alice for whom Scarlett had painted *Crowns*. And it was *Crowns* she blamed for this screw-up.

Despite knowing all about Scarlett's problem and the cause behind it, Audrey carried on. Probably as a deliberate test of Scarlett's mettle. 'Delightful boy, but very shy, although his fiancée, Summer, has done wonders for his confidence.'

'So, another one bites the dust.'

'It's the curse of being an attractive woman, Scarlett. Other women fear and distrust us, suspicious that we're out to steal their men. Or that their men will want to steal us.'

'I have no designs on stealing anyone or allowing myself to be stolen. All I want is to borrow a body for a while. Male, relatively muscular and of a certain age. He doesn't even have to be attractive, just ... potent. That's not too much to ask, is it?'

'I'm afraid it is when you look like you.'

Scarlett stabbed her fork into a cherry tomato half. This wasn't helping. 'Not something I can change.'

To her relief, they moved on to other topics. Mostly gossip about the arts community in Adelaide, where Scarlett had lived all her life before moving to Levenham after her breakup with Felix, and where Audrey maintained strong ties through her family's Wallace Foundation charitable trust.

'What are you going to do if you don't find him?' asked Audrey as they readied to leave.

'I don't know.' Scarlett stared at the street. 'Paint another *Crowns* in the hope it'll cancel the curse?'

'The only curse is the fantasy one in your mind. I suggest you try the livestock exchange. Sales are every Wednesday. You're bound to come across a dishy farmer or stock agent there.'

'Maybe. Or maybe I'll keep painting Jed. Not the same, but ...' She lifted her hands.

'Oh, do stop the misery act. It's very unbecoming.' Perhaps realising she'd gone too far, she patted Scarlett's shoulder. 'Chin up. You'll find your man soon.'

Scarlett hoped she was right. Time was running out.

With Audrey due at the Council Chambers for a meeting and nothing better to do than search for her man model, Scarlett escorted her companion across Civic Park to the historic building. The park's shady trees protected them from the burning sun. After almost a week of mild temperatures, another filthy heatwave had hit the district yesterday, shooting the mercury up to forty degrees. Today was slightly less but still sweltering, with the weather bureau predicting more to come.

The heat had brought out the roses. Shades of pinks, reds, oranges, purples, yellows and creams. Unfurling buds and fat double blooms with velvety petals. Even the bush bases were colourful, thanks to plantings of petunias. Any other time the hues and textures would have excited Scarlett; now she simply felt sweaty, irritated and empty.

She farewelled Audrey with a kiss and trudged back to the restaurant, where she'd left her car in the small carpark behind. Heat haze rose from its sticky asphalt. Even more heat throbbed from the concrete wall of the adjoining building. Her little hatchback's red metallic duco shone like hot steel. Scarlett dreaded to think what the interior was like.

A ute with a fridge unit on the back and a 'Sam's Dairy' logo stencilled on the side was pulled up at the rear of the restaurant, close to the kitchen. One side of the fridge unit's double doors was open and a man with a piece of folded paper between his teeth was dragging a blue crate filled with plastic milk bottles towards him from the inside.

Scarlett's walk slowed, then stopped, her heart thudding.

The man hoisted the crate with a grunt, biceps and shoulders bulging beneath the fabric of his tan-coloured polo shirt. His skin was finely sheened—with sweat or sunscreen, she couldn't tell—and glowed soft gold in the sun. Light-brown curls tipped with copper caressed his stubbled jaw. With a shove of his shoulder, he closed the fridge unit's door and disappeared into the restaurant's rear entrance.

Scarlett's mouth opened, closed, then opened again. A delicious shiver shot through her and she shook herself a little. Calm, she needed calm. It had been a short glimpse. Not enough time to judge properly, and the lack of wedding ring meant nothing.

But she knew. Oh, how she knew. The flutters inside her were so strong, she was in danger of winging skywards at any moment.

She'd found her model man. And he was perfect.

THREE

SAM'S MOUTH was sweet with the Greek custard slice Kai had insisted he try. Sam could never resist the treats the chef pushed on him when he dropped off the restaurant's order. The bloke could really cook, and Sam loved tasting where his milk and cream ended up. It made his heart swell.

He stepped into the sunshine, glanced at the sky and grimaced. The sun was well past its zenith. A breakdown on his small bottling plant that morning had made him late with his deliveries. Again. The second-hand unit was costing him too much downtime, but he was reluctant to invest in a new one. It'd be a major expense, requiring finance, some remodelling if he bought a larger capacity plant, and while Sam's Dairy was growing, he'd seen too many small businesses go broke from over-capitalising too early.

A thought for later, when he'd finished his rounds.

He strode for his ute, pausing at its rear to properly secure the fridge unit doors. As he fastened the main latch, prickles crept over his back and neck. The sort he some-times experienced on the farm late at night, and which usually turned out to be a fox or some other animal eyeing him through the darkness. He turned. A woman was watching him. A very attractive, vaguely familiar woman.

She smiled in a way that brought the blue sky down around his ears.

Anchored in place like a total dork, Sam smiled back.

The woman approached, green eyes held wide, smile still in place. A bit weird considering he didn't know her. At least, Sam didn't think he did. Surely, he'd recognise someone like *her*.

Despite the heat, she was wearing black cargo pants and boots, but it was the green ribbed cotton singlet that caught his attention, the way it suctioned to her skin and amplified the shapes of her waist and breasts, and showed off the straightness of her shoulders. Her hair was long and dark and wavy. And oh, that face. Delicate and pale, like a doll's, yet she wasn't young. Around his age, he guessed. Late twenties, early thirties. Unless ...

A tingle of nervousness infected him. He glanced towards the street, then at the kitchen door before focusing on her again. Like many country towns, Levenham had its share of ice—crystal meth—addicts. They could be unpredictable, violent. He checked her hands in case she was hiding a knife. Nothing.

She stopped a few feet from him, gaze raking his body, and let out a long sigh. 'You're perfect.'

Sam blinked. *Okay.* He wasn't expecting that.

'Er ... thanks.' He scratched his head, watching her closely. With that wide-eyed wonder, she looked more than a bit nutty. Beautiful, mind, but with more than a touch of crazy going on.

She stepped sideways and assessed him with her head tilted and those plump doll lips pursed, then she circled to his other side and repeated the inspection. Her hands flickered here and there, as if she was measuring him or wanted to touch.

'Can I … um, help you?' he said.

'Oh, yes. You can help.' A grown woman's voice, thank God. A bit breathless, but definitely not a prematurely aged teen.

'Okay. Good.' He scratched his head again. 'How?'

Her gaze met his. 'By being you.'

Not helpful.

'Right.'

She stepped even closer. Sam gave the kitchen another glance. He was pretty sure he could take her on if she decided to attack, but it'd be easier to leg it inside. Only cowards hurt women.

He wondered what she was high on. Maybe not ice. Maybe heroin, or those opioid painkillers that had been in the news lately. Unlikely though. She looked too healthy for a junkie and her arms were clean of track marks. Not that he knew what they looked like but he could guess they wouldn't be like her arms, which were pale and smooth and unscarred. Maybe cannabis was her go. A garden-variety pothead.

Why someone so gorgeous would want to waste herself on drugs was beyond him. Life offered better highs, if you treated it right.

She breathed out another long sigh. 'You are so, so perfect.'

'Look,' he said, trying to keep his tone friendly, 'I'm flattered you think so, and normally I'd be more than happy to stick around to hear that a few more times, but I have deliveries to make.' He spread his hands and shrugged. 'Sorry.'

The apology seemed to snap her out of whatever doped-up trance she was in. Her gaze cleared and she straightened. The smile tweaking her cupid's bow mouth now seemed more amused than crazy.

'Of course. Sorry. Don't mind me, I was having a moment.' She thrust out her hand. 'I'm Scarlett Ash.'

Sam shook it automatically. 'Sam Greenwood.'

'Sorry again for the weirdness. I couldn't help myself. I've been looking for you everywhere and then, suddenly, there you are.' She grinned and held her clenched hands beneath her jaw, a little of the crazy returning. 'I can't wait.'

'Wait for what?'

'You.'

'Yeah, okay.' Why did the most gorgeous girl he'd met in ages have to be a crackpot? Talk about unfair. 'It was nice to meet you, Scarlett, but I really have to go.'

'No.' She reached out as if to grab his arm, then pulled back and closed her eyes for a second. 'I'm doing this badly. Wine at lunchtime.' She shook her head. 'Silly. But I didn't expect to …' She puffed out her cheeks and growled. 'I'm doing it again.'

Sam watched on, intrigued.

'I'm a professional artist, a painter. A very good one, and I've been looking for a life-model to sit for me. I'd very much like for it to be you.'

'Me? A model?' Sam snorted. 'You might want to get those pretty eyes of yours checked.'

Sam knew he wasn't a bad-looking rooster, but no way was he model material. His nose was a bit big and kinked to the left thanks to being hit by a stray surfboard, and most of the time his salt-damaged hair looked like Medusa's. At five feet eleven, he wasn't particularly tall, either. His shoulders were good, he supposed, from years of swimming and surfing, and his mum and sisters reckoned he had nice hazel eyes, not that he could see it. To Sam, they had all the colours of a swamp. Maybe a sunlit one when the light shone right, but still a swamp.

Good bloke, yeah. Model, no.

Tempting, though, if it meant spending time with Scarlett, because, man, she was something. When she wasn't acting crazy, that was.

'My eyes are fine. Look, I appreciate you probably think I'm nuts, but I'm serious. You have all the qualities I've been searching for. It's legitimate employment at award wages. A couple of days a week for a few hours, at a time that suits you. Interested?'

Yeah, Sam was interested, but not because of the money or being painted or whatever she planned to do. If he did this gig, it'd be because of her. He rubbed his jaw, eyeing her and trying to figure out whatever was nagging at his brain. Sam had never met Scarlett, yet he couldn't shed this feeling of familiarity.

She'd gone big-eyed again, lips parted and her expression filled with desperation. What was with that? There were plenty of blokes who'd sit for someone like her. Who wouldn't want to? She was a stunner.

He gave himself a mental smack. What was he thinking? No matter how beautiful Scarlett Ash was, Sam had more than enough on his plate, and there was the little matter of the crazy.

It might have been a while between girls, but even Sam wasn't up for that.

She pointed at his ute and the 'Sam's Dairy' sign. 'This is your business?'

He nodded.

'You're a dairy farmer?'

'Yeah.'

'My neighbours are dairy farmers. You might know them, Jed and Faye Michalski? My studio is in their old dairy. Perhaps it's not far from your farm?'

The faint recognition that he'd been feeling this entire encounter suddenly solidified. 'I know who you are now,' he said, waggling his finger at her. 'You're *that* artist.'

Her gaze sharpened and her voice turned low. '*That* artist?'

'Yeah. My mum has one of your paintings. It's …' He scrambled to think of a polite way of putting it. While the painting was pretty out there, it was clear even to him that the rendering was of a woman kneeling on a bed with her naked bum to the viewer. A dark-haired woman, come to think of it. A dark-haired woman with pale skin and green …

Holy shit.

'Very bright,' he said finally, and winced at the schoolboy high edge in his voice. 'Nice.'

'Nice?'

'Yeah, in a …' Bloody hell. His cheeks were burning and it wasn't because of the sun, although that wasn't helping. 'Bedroom kind of way.'

'Ah.' She laughed. 'I won't ask which one it is. I can tell from your face what series it's from.'

Good idea. He wouldn't know how to describe it, anyway. He didn't even want to *think* about it right now.

Sam's back pocket vibrated. He extracted his phone and checked the screen, then put it back again. A mate wanting to know if he wanted to go for a surf after milking. No chance. His day had started as ordinary and descended into crap.

Which reminded him, it would get even crappier if he didn't get a wriggle on.

'I really have to go.'

'Yes, of course.' She reached into the pocket of her cargo pants, extracted a card and handed it to him. 'Call me. I'm serious about you modelling and I really don't know what I'll do if you say no.'

He took the card and inspected it. On one side was a painting, like his mum's in style, but this time with the dark-haired figure dressed—mostly—and sitting cross-legged with a long-stemmed black rose held diagonally across her chest. She was surrounded by rainbows of colour that contrasted, at least it seemed so to Sam, with her sad face.

He flipped the card over. Plain text revealed her name, email address and phone number.

Scarlett curved her hand around the outside of his and squeezed. 'Please call?'

Sam swallowed. How could he refuse? He was a well-raised man and it'd be rude to leave her hanging, even if the answer was no. 'Yeah, okay.'

Her smile brought the blue sky back around his head. 'Thank you.' She squeezed his hand again and gave it a short shake. 'Thank you!'

She stepped back, beaming at him, and suddenly he was no longer average Sam. He was special Sam. Perfect Sam.

Maybe even model Sam.

FOUR

SAM FINISHED his deliveries in a state of bemusement. Scarlett Ash had been something else. A model. Him. He'd laugh, except she'd been dead serious. And now his libido was dead serious about taking up the offer.

He needed to get a grip. He didn't have time to surf let alone model, and at least surfing kept him fit and cleared his head. What would modelling do except eat into the precious little spare time he had? It was probably batshit boring, too.

Although, if this afternoon's encounter was anything to go by, any time with Scarlett would be far from boring.

Sam rubbed his head. He needed her out of there. Just because she was gorgeous didn't mean she wasn't completely off her rocker. Or doped up to the eyeballs on something. He didn't need that worry in his life. The bottling plant was bad enough.

He found a car space in front of the old jail, and with a bottle of milk in his hand, jogged across the road to the limestone-and-red-dolomite building that housed his mother's solicitor's office, a short distance from Levenham's police station and courthouse complex.

'Hey, Leanne,' said Sam as he passed by reception and headed to the kitchenette to dump the milk in the fridge. Leanne smiled and continued typing, no doubt transcribing from whatever was filtering through the headphones she wore. She'd been working for his mum since Sam could remember and she'd watched him grow up from boyhood.

'Is she busy?' he mouthed on his return.

Leanne glanced at the switch and shook her head. 'Go on in. She's just off the phone.'

Sam wandered up the corridor. The door to his mum's office was ajar. He rapped his knuckles on it and poked his head around the corner. 'It's me.'

Karen Patzel lifted her head from what she was reading and smiled. 'Hello, you.' She glanced at her smartwatch. 'You're a bit late today.'

Sam planted himself into a chair opposite her desk. 'Bottling plant went bung again.' He nodded at the paper she held. 'Nothing too nasty, I hope.'

'Yes, unfortunately.'

Sam knew not to probe further. His mother specialised in family law and some of the cases she worked on were ugly, especially those involving children. Fortunately, those were few, but even one was too many.

'Here's hoping it's resolved quickly, then.'

'Unlikely, but we can hope.' She tilted her head, eyes sharpening. His mum was an attractive woman; hazel-eyed, like he was, and with straight shoulder-length brown hair, lightly touched with grey. At work she was Karen Patzel, sleek, besuited solicitor. On the farm, she was Karen Greenwood, daggy dairy-farming wife and mum of three. The contrast never ceased to make Sam smile. 'What's up?'

'Nothing, really.'

She arched an eyebrow.

Sam laughed. 'All right. I've just had an offer from one of your clients.' At his mum's expression, he hurried on. She'd encountered more than her fair share of addicts and even dealers in her time, and once, dramatically, had acted for a murderer, although in that case the accused was more victim. 'Nothing like that. It was that artist, Scarlett Ash. The one who did the painting in your bedroom. She wants me to model for her.' He lifted his chin and puffed out his chest. 'She says I'm perfect.'

'Does she now?'

Sam grinned. 'Uh-huh.'

His mum continued to study him. Sam couldn't tell what was going on behind that clever gaze. Karen Patzel was well-practised at keeping her thoughts to herself. 'Are you going to say yes?'

He shrugged. 'I don't really have the time.'

'But you want to.'

'Hard to say no to someone who thinks you're perfect.'

'Mmm.' She picked up a pen and rolled it between her fingers. 'And the fact that she's very attractive has nothing to do with it?'

'Not a thing.'

She smiled. 'Liar.'

Sam slapped his hand on his chest. 'Who me?'

Her smile eased a little and she rested the end of the pen against her bottom lip. 'She's a nice girl. Smart. Tough, too, and very talented.'

'Not crazy, then?'

'Scarlett? No, far from it. Why on earth would you think that?'

'I did mention that she thinks I'm perfect, didn't I?' He turned serious. 'Not a druggie or anything, is she?'

'Not that I'm aware of. Although, I haven't had dealings with her for a while.' She frowned and bounced the pen off her lip. 'Are you seriously contemplating her offer?'

'Why? Shouldn't I?'

'That's entirely up to you.' She bounced the pen a few more times. 'You do realise what life-modelling entails?'

'Yeah.' At least he thought he did. 'A lot of sitting still, I imagine. Trying not to fidget.' Sam lifted an arm and tightened his bicep. 'Flexing a couple of muscles.'

'Life-models pose nude.'

Sam's jaw dropped. He swallowed. 'Nude?'

'Yes, nude.'

'As in no clothes at all?'

'Yes, my darling son. That's what nude usually means.'

He sat back and dragged his hand down his face. Not only did Scarlett think him perfect, she wanted him naked. 'Holy shit.'

'Holy shit indeed.'

'Well, then,' said Sam, chuckling as he stood up. 'Good thing I'm not shy.'

Summer Sunday afternoons in Levenham couldn't be more typically Australian. The streak of hot weather had continued into the weekend, tempting flocks of locals to the beach. The carparks servicing Admella Beach and Port Andrews were full, the shorelines made colourful with umbrellas, towels, coolers topped with ice, beer and soft drinks, and kids in shiny, protective sunsuits.

Normally, Sam would be right alongside them in board

shorts, rashie and thongs, his skin slathered with sunscreen. Instead, he was driving to Jed Michalski's place with his stomach in knots and his mouth as dry as the parched paddocks surrounding him.

'Idiot,' he muttered to himself.

It was stupid to be so nervous. When he'd asked Scarlett on the phone about nuding up, she'd laughed and told him not to worry. They might not even get to that stage. Sam hadn't known whether to be disappointed or relieved. The idea of getting naked in front of Scarlett was kind of exciting, but she had made it sound like she didn't care either way.

As dumb as it sounded, and given he'd met her once and then when she was freaky weird, he wanted her to care.

That it was business was hammered home when she emailed through an employment agreement for him to sign. Sam had read it with surprise. There was stuff about use of his image and claims and whatever, things that had never once crossed his mind about what the job might entail. He'd showed it to his mum, who had read it carefully then explained the clauses.

'It's all reasonable, in my opinion,' she'd said, passing it back to him. 'Just make sure you've properly thought through the consequences.'

Sam had signed the document and sent it back. If Scarlett wanted to put him on display, she could go for it. He had nothing to be ashamed of, and if his mum's artwork was anything to go by, he'd be hard to recognise, anyway. Sam wasn't about to let on about the gig either, in case any of his mates decided they too were perfect and attempted to cut his grass.

The Michalskis' farm was eighteen or so kilometres from Heatherbrae, his parents' place. Where Heatherbrae hugged the coast and sprawled over what was essentially reclaimed swamp, the Michalskis' was inland on fertile grey-brown loams over limestone. It was rich country; the sort of land Sam would love to farm but would never be able to afford.

He passed the giant shed housing Jed's sixty-unit rotary dairy and tried not to feel jealous. Heatherbrae wasn't making them rich, but it did all right, and he was happy working with his dad, Les, and their part-timer, Malcolm. Together they made a good team, and his parents had always been supportive of Sam's separate Jersey dairy operation, even if it did mean a lot more work and extra accounting.

Not far beyond the shed a lane appeared, along with a much smaller solid limestone shed sporting a colourful blue steel roof. Sam indicated and drove in, bouncing in his seat as the ute hit a deep pothole. He pulled onto a concrete apron, leaving the engine and aircon running as he took a moment to calm his nerves and take in the impressive sight that was Scarlett's studio and home.

Not bad for what was once a walk-through dairy.

According to gossip, the whole place had been gutted and renovated at not inconsiderable cost. Usually, these old dairies were left to rot or used for storing junk, but Faye had come up with the idea of creating farmstay accommodation and Jed had gone along with it. The farmstay hadn't lasted. Probably because the location wasn't that scenic. Its proximity to the new dairy wouldn't have helped either. Milking started early and cows could be noisy buggers, not to mention smelly, and dairies attracted flies in droves.

Not something that bothered Scarlett, it seemed.

Sam killed the engine and stepped out into the heat, and was immediately accosted by flies. He scanned the structure, wondering where the front door was located. The conversion was basically a stone rectangle with a pitched roof. The large opening where Jed's herd had once shuffled their way into stalls was now completely enclosed by windows, privacy and light controlled by internal plantation shutters.

A double carport had been built on the western side. A small red hatchback that he assumed was Scarlett's was parked underneath. His eyebrows lifted at the make. This painting lark must be all right if she could afford a Lexus.

A flash of movement behind the shutters caught his attention. Scarlett. Sam's chest tightened and the skin across the back of his neck contracted in anticipation. He told himself not to be such a nong, but the nerves wouldn't stop.

A screen door swung open into the carport, and Scarlett stepped out, her doll-like face radiant and smiling.

'Sam, you made it.'

'I did.' Sam cleared his throat and tried for nonchalance, nodding at the dairy. 'I'd heard about Jed's farmstay project, but this is the first time I've been here.' He nodded again, then realised what a tool he was for doing so. As if Scarlett needed or would even care about his approval. 'Impressive for an old cow shed.'

'It suits me.' She beckoned and held open the screen door. 'Don't keep standing in the sun, come inside.'

Sam had expected something like a two-bedroom flat. Instead, he found one vast timber-floored room ringed with colour. There were paintings propped everywhere—stacks of the things, balanced against one another like dominoes. In the space closest to the windows, what looked like a giant lightweight canvas tarpaulin had been spread across the floor. An empty easel stood at one end, a paint- and brush-laden trolley next to it, along with a grey aluminium outdoor lounger on which a workbook was casually tossed.

'Nice,' he said, unable to think of any other description.

'A mess, is what you mean.' Scarlett lifted her hands from her sides and flopped them back down again. She was in similar clothes as when he met her on Thursday—black cargo pants and heavy boots, although this time her singlet top was bright red. 'I've been too excited to tidy.'

Excited? That made two of them.

'Would you like a cold drink?' She pointed to a kitchen area where a teapot shared bench space with a shiny kettle, microwave, pod coffee machine and a bottle of some sort of clear spirit. Vodka? Gin? Maybe that's where the weirdness came from. 'Or some tea or coffee?'

'Water would be great.'

Sam scanned the rest of the room as she fetched the drink. A queen-size bed with a mussed-up doona on top occupied the south-west side of the room. A plain white melamine wardrobe with drawers in its base sat to its left, a small bedside table topped with a shiny chrome reading lamp on its right. Next to the table was an open door, the flash of white tile and bright light suggesting a bathroom in what he guessed was once the wash and tank room. Like the kitchen, the bedroom quarter was neat, apart from the doona, with no clothes or dirty dishes strewn about. It was a strange contrast to the rest of the room, and he wondered what that said about her.

He sauntered over to the wall of propped canvases. The colours were incredible, vivid and almost glittery, as if a series of jewellers' trays had been upended and swirled about. Sam glanced at Scarlett and found her watching him as she poured water.

He gestured at the paintings. 'May I?'

'Sure. Knock yourself out.'

He crouched to flick through a layer. The first was a painting of a woman standing in a whirlpool of colour that made him think of the oily rainbows that sometimes appeared in spilled fuel. The woman was strangely proportioned—her head overlarge, her body thin but with dramatically defined muscles. She had a sheet draped over one shoulder, her neck long and stretched as she stared at something behind her.

The next painting was of a green-eyed, dark-haired woman, her body pale and arched and surrounded by alien plant life that was creeping hungrily towards her. One arm was lifted as though beckoning the viewer to join her in her fantasy world.

Sam swallowed and flicked quickly to the next painting, and wished he hadn't. The scene was similar, but this time the woman's eyes were closed and her lips open on an erotic sigh. If that wasn't disturbing enough, her thighs had been eased apart by plant tendrils that had wrapped around her ankles. In the swirly green and browns of the surrounding forest, hooded eyes glowed.

Sam jerked upright and shoved his hands deep into his jeans' pockets. Now was not a good time to be thinking about naked women, and especially not a naked Scarlett.

Scarlett was leaning against the bench, a glass of water in her hand and laughter all over her face. 'Find anything you like?'

'No. I mean yes.' He shook his head. What the hell could he say? 'They're ... er ... very bright.'

'They are. Bright with the power of the feminine.'

'Yeah.' Sam wasn't about to disagree with her. They had power all right. One look and he'd been damn-near reduced to a quivering fool. A turned-on quivering fool.

She laughed and crossed to hand him his water. Sam accepted it gratefully and took a long slurp. He wished his nerves would stop ringing. He was a grown man, for God's sake.

'So, ah, what do you need me to do?'

'Just sit.' She indicated the lounger. 'Sit and relax.'

'Clothes on?'

'Yes, Sam. Clothes on.'

Good. Togging off right now would be seriously embarrassing.

She removed the workbook from the lounger and propped it on the easel, then wheeled over a stool from beneath the kitchen bench. Straddling the stool, she adjusted the easel downwards until it was level with her chest and turned her back to arrange some equipment on the trolley table.

Sam sank his bum onto the lounger. He draped his arms over his knees, then thought better of it and rested them alongside his thighs. Feeling awkward, he shifted again, the lounger making disconcerting squeaking noises as it moved under his weight.

'I don't know how to sit,' said Sam, when he caught Scarlett eyeing him.

'Any way you like. Just be comfortable.' She was kneading one-handed a ball of grey stuff that looked like plasticine. 'Putty rubber,' she said, lobbing it to him. 'For erasing charcoal.'

It was grey and dirty looking. He tossed it back, Scarlett catching it with ease.

She set it aside and picked up a dark-grey stick. 'This is vine charcoal. Messy stuff, but good for free-flowing sketches.' This time she handed it over rather than throwing it.

Sam inspected it and passed it back, rubbing his fingers where the charcoal had left dust. 'You don't use paints?'

'Not in the preliminary stages.' She whirled on her stool to face him and leaned slightly forward with her hands rested on her knees. 'The point of sketching is to get a feel for your essence. To study and eventually capture it.'

'My essence?'

'Yes. Your ...' She lifted a hand and waved it over his length. 'Strength and masculinity. The very things that sang to me when I first saw you.'

'Right.' It all sounded very arty-farty, but no matter, Sam liked the sound of her language. Strength and masculinity. *Yeah, baby*.

'It's unlikely to happen today. I just hope ...' Sucking on her lip, she regarded the blank page, then shook her head and smiled at him. 'The most important thing is for you to relax and be yourself.'

Like that would be easy. He still had half a hard-on and his brain kept dodging back to the lusty plant painting. Scarlett's strength-and-masculinity statement had only added to the pressure. Being himself when he felt completely out of his depth would be impossible.

Yet that sucking of her lip suggested worry or doubt, and Sam wasn't about to let this beautiful girl down. Even if she was a bit nuts.

'I'll do my best.'

'In that case, Sam my model man, we will begin.'

FIVE

SCARLETT HESITATED with her hand over the pastel paper. The charcoal felt unstable in her fingers, as if it could snap at any moment.

She forced her hand to relax. There was no need to be nervous. She'd sketched dozens of people in her career—men, women, children. The aged, the young. Once, she'd spent a wonderful day in a home for special-needs children and young adults drawing portraits, and she'd gained more from them and their ready smiles than they could have possibly gained from her simple sketches.

Sam should be a cinch. Yet, here she was, tremble-handed and with sweat edging her hairline while he man-sprawled on Jed's outdoor lounge chair like he did this kind of thing every day.

She had to make this work. He was *it*. She knew it within her bones. The man who would coax her imagination out of the dark, dank hole into which it had sunk, who would reignite her love of creation and inspire her talent to even greater heights.

She studied him again. He was staring at her stacked

canvases, two fine lines edging his inner brows and one corner of his mouth lifted. Not in a smile, more in puzzlement.

That Sam had even turned up surprised her. Scarlett had hoped, but it was far from a done deal, not after her bizarre behaviour in the restaurant carpark. It had been the shock of the unexpected that had made her act the way she had. And desperation. She needed someone like him so badly it had become an albatross around her neck, weighing her not only psychologically but physically. Disturbing her sleep, stretching her days with anxiety. Making her itch with nerves that she wouldn't recover in time for her residency.

That she wouldn't recover at all.

Encountering him in a carpark, of all places, was like being struck by a shaft of heavenly light. It had left her breathless, featherweight, awed. So awed she could barely string words together. Scarlett could hardly blame him for being spooked. She'd spooked herself.

Hearing his voice when he'd called on Friday night— deep and a little gravelly—had shot her heart racing. She'd answered his questions with her fists clenched, wishing, hoping. Then he'd told her to email the agreement through and she'd done so, still not believing it could happen. He'd sent it back the following day with a note saying, 'See you Sunday.' Even then, it wasn't until he'd parked in her drive that she'd run from the windows, punching the air with joy, and trampolined up and down on her bed like a child before bouncing off and racing to the door, where she had composed herself back to cool professionalism before she'd stepped out in case he changed his mind and bolted.

Now he was here, and she was bubbling with excitement and fear.

What if it didn't work?

As if sensing her scrutiny, his gaze shot to hers and he smiled. 'Sorry, should I be looking at you?'

'Up to you. Like I said, do whatever you feel makes you the most relaxed and that you can hold for a few minutes.'

His lips pursed as he considered, then he shifted onto his side and rested his head on his elbow, his legs stretched out and his focus on her. 'This okay?'

Scarlett hesitated. Having models watch her work had never bothered her prior to today, but that was before *Crowns* had stolen her mojo. She set her shoulders. Stuff *Crowns*. This would not beat her. 'It's fine.'

Scarlett held up the length of charcoal and measured his brow line. Sam had a nice brow. He had a nice every-thing. Not conventionally good-looking—he was too asym-metrical for that—but attractive all the same, and with very appealing shoulders.

She sighted a few more proportions, aware she was procrastinating yet reluctant to commit charcoal to paper. His eyes followed her with interest. She lowered her hand and regarded the blank sheet.

One stroke was all she needed. One line to start, then the others would follow.

Still she stared. Sweat gathered at the top of her spine and prickled her scalp. The air felt dense and stagnant and short of oxygen. Her lungs tightened.

'Scarlett?'

She glanced at him. The lines between his brows had deepened further.

'You okay?'

She nodded.

'Sure?'

'Yes.' Except she wasn't. She was terrified.

She swallowed, her throat sticking. She could feel Sam's gaze darting over her, his concern and curiosity tensing the already thick air. He must think her crazy, which wouldn't be far off the truth right now. This stupid block was making her feel crazy.

She wasn't. She was talented and smart, and this was just a bloody preliminary drawing. If it was crap, stiff. She'd do another and another until the magic returned.

Inhaling a deep breath, she began to sketch.

At first her lines were short, her fear and damaged confidence making them vague and choppy, but as she progressed the second nature of the activity took over. Slowly, her ruler-straight mouth lost its pensiveness, and muscles that had been stiff with tension loosened.

As she relaxed, so did Sam. His frown lines disappeared and his mouth parted slightly. Light glittered in his hazel eyes; little golden sparks against the olive and raw umber and made more intense by a frame of thick, long lashes. She hadn't noticed that when they met. Scarlett had been too intent on the strength and proportions of his body, but Sam had lovely eyes that spoke of intelligence and, she thought, kindness.

Her job was to capture that. And more.

If only it were so easy.

'Give it time,' she muttered, flipping over to a clean page. While the first sketch was perfectly competent, it lacked soul. The next would be better.

It wasn't.

Growling, Scarlett snapped the sheet over and started again. Swift strokes to outline his body, a faintly sketched oval for his face. Lines to position his arms and legs. Walking the charcoal over the page, taking it, and her, on a journey of discovery.

Other than the scratch of charcoal, the occasional squeak from the lounger as Sam shifted a muscle, or the buzz of a fly as it frantically headbutted a window, there was little noise. The constant whir of the ceiling fans had long faded into the background. Sometimes, in the distance, a dog barked or a cow lowed. Determined to bully her creativity into life, Scarlett ignored them. She outlined, shaded, smudged and rubbed, her frustration growing with every movement. It wasn't that her work was bad, it was that it wasn't good. The charcoal produced no journey, no revelations. It was merely dust on a page.

Scarlett didn't do average. Average was anathema. Yet that seemed to be her norm now.

Muttering, she flicked the page over to a clean one and started again.

It took a long while before she realised the lounger squeaks were getting more frequent. She tried to push through the interruptions. It had taken five sheets but finally something was stirring inside her. A glimmer of creativity that was urging Scarlett to exaggerate her lines. Make the figure bigger. Braver. Active. Not a man reclined; rather, one on the cusp of rising. His power latent and shimmering.

The lounger squeaked again. Scarlett shot Sam a look.

'Sorry,' he said, his teeth gritted. 'I didn't mean to move.'

Scarlett glanced at the microwave clock and her eyes widened. Had she been working that long? Poor Sam, and on his first sitting.

She pushed away from the easel, her palms raised. 'God, Sam, it's me who should be apologising. I had no idea I'd gotten so lost. You must be as stiff as a board. Or bored stiff.' She stood and held out a hand for him to grab.

He took it and levered himself up. 'Not stiff. Just

finding it hard to keep still. I'm not used to lazing around. Too much to do usually.' He walked to the easel and studied the sketch, rubbing his chin.

Scarlett's stomach muscles tensed.

He looked back at her and scanned her face, then across to her stacked works and back at the sketch. 'It's different to what I thought you'd do.'

She'd expected praise. That's what most inexperienced sitters did—gushed about how marvellous her work was regardless of artistic merit, afraid of causing offence if they didn't laud it. Sam's inspection was intense and more than a little disconcerting, as if he knew the work lacked soul. As if he knew *she* was lacking.

Defensiveness made her words taut. 'What did you expect?'

'I'm not sure.' Sam glanced again at her paintings. 'Something not this life-like maybe.' He returned his focus to the drawing. 'Except it's not really life-like, either. It's me but not me.' He shook his head. 'That probably makes zero sense.'

'No. It makes perfect sense. Life-drawing isn't about being photographic, it's about capturing the subject's inner nature, their strengths and vulnerabilities.' She folded her arms. 'I wish I could say I've done that here, but I haven't.'

'Why do you think that?'

'It lacks energy. There's no ... essence. No real indication of the inner you.'

'We only met a couple of days ago. You don't know anything about me. How can you expect to be able to show it?'

He was right. Scarlett didn't know him. All she had was her uncanny sixth sense that he was what she needed.

She rubbed her shoulder where an ache had set in.

Perhaps she was going about this the wrong way. Rushing the process in her search for a cure. Her feminine series had been mostly self-portraits, while her last commission had been Audrey Wallace, whom she'd known for a long time. Sam was a stranger.

Scarlett glanced at the clock again. She had just under an hour remaining of their agreed time. 'How are you feeling? Not too stiff?'

'I'm fine.'

'Take a break for a few minutes, then we'll go again.' She pointed to the bathroom. 'Toilet's through there, if you need. Can I get you another drink?'

'That'd be great, thanks.' He shoved his hands in his pockets and strolled a lap of the room, eyeing her artworks as he went but not crouching to look through. He was probably too scared. Not that Scarlett could blame him. By some fate, Sam had chosen a stack of her most erotic self-portraits. It could have been worse. Sam could have leafed through her sketchbook of Audrey Wallace nudes. The thought made her smile. Audrey would have loved that.

'What are you smiling at?'

'Oh.' Scarlett flushed and quickly opened the fridge for the water jug. 'Nothing much. Nudes mostly.'

His eyebrows shot up.

'Not you.' Although now that she thought about it, maybe that would inspire something. Scarlett imagined lots of interesting shapes lurked beneath Sam's white polo shirt and khaki work pants.

'Shame.'

'Keen to get undressed?'

Sam laughed. He had a pleasant laugh. Genuine and easy flowing, like he did it often. 'No. But in case you hadn't noticed, it's stinking hot.'

'Sorry about that. I'll turn up the fans and open the windows. You can entertain yourself watching flies crawl over the screens. It's a bit horror movie around here, the way they swarm.' She feigned a shudder. 'Scary.'

'They're not that bad.'

'Trust me, they are.'

He raised a shoulder. 'Flies love dairy farms.'

'Why is that?' she asked, pouring herself some water. 'I mean, I know there's lots of manure around, but they're insane right now.'

'They're always rotten in the summer. They're attracted by the moisture.' He peered out the south window, beyond which ran the lane, and further out Jed's centre pivot stretched its arms and made the irrigated pasture beneath an emerald oasis. 'They're not too bad here. I've seen much worse.' He wandered back for his water glass and drank. 'Jed's a good operator. Your biggest problem is location. Too close to the lane and shed.' Sam took another long draught, his Adam's apple bobbing as he swallowed. 'What made you choose here?'

She shrugged. 'It was cheap. It also had the right amount of space and light.'

He gazed around, nodding. 'Mum said you're from Adelaide.'

'How would your mum know that?'

'She's done work for you. Karen Patzel?'

Scarlett's jaw went slack. 'The solicitor?'

'The one and only.'

'Let me guess, she uses her maiden name.'

'She does. She's a modern woman, my mum.'

'I can imagine.'

Sam grinned at that. 'You don't know the half of it.'

No, she likely didn't, but Scarlett was curious to find

out. Karen Patzel had impressed her with her professionalism and solidarity. From the moment they'd shaken hands, Scarlett had felt Karen was on her side, that she could be trusted. With his easy smile and good manners, Sam gave off a similar vibe.

'So, that's how you've seen my work before. I've been wondering about that.' Scarlett studied him. The resemblance was obvious now. Same eyes, same cheekbones. She shook her head. 'Funny world.'

'Yeah.' He finished his drink and placed the glass in the sink, then glanced at his watch. 'Guess we'd better get back to it?'

'I guess we'd better.'

SIX

WITH EVERY PASSING MINUTE, Sam's fascination with Scarlett grew. Her focus was absolute, almost trance-like. Her glances like darts, hitting him sharp and fast before bouncing back to the page, her arm in constant motion as she captured her vision of him. Whatever that was.

How she caught anything with those lightning-fast peeks was beyond him. Sam may as well be a hunk of meat, hung for her appreciation. Which would be annoying if she weren't so extraordinary. Or paying for his time.

There was no question that Scarlett was good. The final drawing from the first session was incredible. Weird, but amazing and more than a bit flattering.

She'd created an over-inflated version of him. Taken his basic structure and remoulded it until he appeared like a Renaissance sculpture coming to life, all ripples and contained power. A sculpture about to rear up and do ... violence? God, he hoped not. If that was what she saw in him, he needed to change something. Fast.

Either that, or she really was on drugs.

At least now Scarlett seemed happier than during the

first sitting. Then, he'd perceived hesitancy, maybe even reluctance, and for a scary moment Sam had thought it was him, that she'd decided he wasn't perfect, after all. Then she'd settled into her work and he'd figured everything was okay. Eased by the quiet and comfort of the lounger, his mind had drifted to his bottling plant problem and the pros and cons of upgrading.

Could he afford it? Probably not, but a point would come when he couldn't afford not to upgrade, and he was feeling increasingly like that would be happening soon. Every week his business was growing, thanks to happy customers and word of mouth. But how big did he want to get?

A snap of paper as Scarlett flipped over a sheet had cut short his mull. He'd assessed her, noting the scratch of the charcoal as her strokes became harder and darker, the mouth twitches and bitter mutters. The flash of her eyes as she almost snarled at her work, then at him for his restlessness.

Her face was more relaxed now, and the movement of her arm more flowing. Not that Sam knew whether that was good or not, but he figured it had to be better than the jerky motions and growls she was making before.

He smiled as her tongue slipped between her lips and stayed.

'You're smiling.'

He regarded her from beneath a flop of hair. Scarlett had shifted the lounger aside and asked Sam to stand with his hands in his pockets, and his left foot forward and his torso angled slightly. 'I am.'

She continued to sketch.

'Is smiling not allowed?'

She slanted him a look. 'It's fine.'

'I'll keep it up, then.'

For a long while, she said nothing. As promised, Sam kept up his half-smile, but like his pose it was wearing thin. He wanted to scratch, fidget, anything. How long had it been? Five minutes? Ten? The position of his arm and twisted waist prevented him from seeing his watch. Sam attempted a peek at the microwave clock only to find the angle for that was wrong, too. Nor could he amuse himself with watching the sketch form on paper because Scarlett had moved the easel and all Sam could see was the sketch-book's back.

His smile disappeared. This was getting boring. The temperature had risen also; the ceiling fans merely agitating the hot air. He should have gone for a surf, except that would have robbed him of a chance to be with this intriguing woman.

'It's not easy, is it?'

'What?'

'Modelling. I've done it myself.'

'For your self-portraits?'

'Sometimes. I work mostly off photos for those.' More dart-like glances peppered his body, although this time a hint of a smile tipped her doll's mouth upwards in one corner. 'I pose with a camera set up on a time lapse.'

'Right.' What he really meant was *good*. The idea of someone taking nude photos of her didn't sit well with him. Not that Sam had any right to feel that way, but still. Plenty of women suffered exploitation via intimate photographs, as his mother and sisters had pointed out more than once. He wouldn't want Scarlett—or anyone—exposed to that. 'But you've worked as a life-model for others?'

'Not professionally.'

'It's a profession?'

'Of course. Quite a well-paying one.' She pointed the charcoal end at him. 'It's hard work, Sam. As you're discovering. We haven't even got you doing anything difficult yet and you're already twitching like a rabbit.'

Huh. She'd noticed. So much for his stoicism.

She continued to speak as she resumed sketching. 'I shared a house with three other artists when I was at uni. We used to pose for one another. None of us found it easy. Brodie was the worst.' Her gaze turned inwards for a moment, then settled on Sam. 'I think men find it harder. Especially active ones.'

'You studied art at uni?'

She nodded. 'Bachelor of Visual Arts. With honours.'

The news didn't surprise Sam. Honours were usually only open to high-achieving students and even he could see Scarlett had talent. Not only talent but a degree of success, if that Lexus was anything to go by.

'Did you always want to be an artist?'

'Pretty much. Although I had a vague ambition to be a nurse when I was little.'

Sam's mind flooded with an image of Scarlett in a short nurse's uniform. *Yeah, baby.*

'What about you?' She bent close to her work and rubbed, flicked him a look, and, tongue pressed between her lips, rubbed some more. 'Did you always want to be a dairy farmer?'

'Not always. I was a mechanical engineer for a while.'

Her head jerked back. 'Really?'

'Hard to believe?'

She stared at him, gaze unblinking and her brows drawn in a frown. 'No,' she said slowly. 'I don't think it is.'

'What makes you figure that?'

'I don't know.' She transferred her scowl to her work,

made a few strokes, looked at him again and made a few more strokes. 'There's something there …'

Sam wished he could see what she was doing. What was the something she'd noticed? At least she seemed to be looking at him properly now, like he was more than a meaty toy. Maybe he should have pulled the engineer line earlier.

Live and learn, Sammy-boy. Live and learn.

'Why mechanical engineering?'

'I was always good at maths and science, and I really liked tinkering with stuff on the farm. Building things, fixing anything broken. My sisters had both gone to uni and I think Mum and Dad wanted me to at least have a go. Mechanical engineering seemed the most interesting.'

'But it wasn't?'

'For a while. I finished my degree, got a job with a ship-building firm at Williamstown. That's in Melbourne. We worked on Defence projects. It was pretty cool at first, but I missed the farm.' He gave her a cheeky look from beneath his hair. 'I like cows.'

'I should hope so. It'd be a miserable existence if you didn't.' She stood back from her work and eyed it, one arm folded over her breast and tucked under her armpit as she tapped the charcoal against her bottom lip with the other hand.

'Better this time?'

'I think so.'

'Maybe talking helped.'

'Maybe it did.'

He grinned. 'We should do it some more, then.'

'Sam.'

Christ, the way she said his name—husky and a bit schoolmarmish—was a serious turn-on.

'Scarlett?'

'Are you trying to flirt?'

Sam slapped his palm on his chest. 'Wouldn't dream of it.'

'I'm glad to hear that because it won't get you anywhere.'

'It won't?'

'No.'

Bummer.

'You sure? Because I distinctly remember you calling me perfect. More than once.'

Scarlett set down her charcoal and sauntered towards him. Sam's gaze skittered to her breasts and hips. She might not be as tall as one, but the woman could strut better than a supermodel.

She stopped in front of him. Close. Really close. Sam had to brace hard to keep his eyes on her face and stop them from dropping to see if her singlet gaped enough for him to see the top of her breasts.

Her head tipped to one side. 'Do I need to remind you of our contract?'

Contract? Uh-oh.

Sam considered himself a modern, enlightened man—you didn't get to be much else growing up with three strong, smart women watching your every move and pouncing on even the most inadvertent sexism—but from her tone Scarlett seemed to be confusing a harmless flirt with harassment.

Then again, maybe he was harassing her. She was a beautiful woman alone in the countryside with a man she barely knew and who, while not being the giant she'd drawn, was still a well-built bloke.

Shit.

He held up his palms. 'Sorry. My mistake.'

Her gaze remained steady for a long moment. A long

moment when Sam's breath was so tight his lungs threatened to squeak.

'Good,' she said. Then she smiled. A dazzling smile that
made his head all floaty and his good intentions evaporate.
Leaning forward, Scarlett poked his chest, her green eyes
glittery. 'You might be perfect, Sam Greenwood, but you're
not *that* perfect.'

SEVEN

NOT PERFECT. Not perfect. Not perfect.

If Scarlett said it enough, she might begin to believe it.

She huffed out a laugh and softly bounced her head on the fridge door, then held it against the cool surface. Who was she kidding? Sam was lovely.

Lovely, smart and patient. And very attractive in a beachy, surfer-dude kind of way. Worse, he was developing a thing for her.

Which was very flattering and more than a little bit heart-fluttery, but she didn't have the time or emotional space for a man, no matter how not perfect.

With a sigh, she left the fridge and returned to flipping through her sketches. She could see a definite improvement in the later drawings. Her mojo was coming back, although not as fast as she'd like. When she'd first spotted Sam in the carpark, she'd anticipated a great whoosh of imagination the moment she put charcoal to paper. A foolish assumption given how deeply she'd fallen into her creative black hole, but the surge of hope she'd felt had left her euphoric, and on a high of silly emotion.

Emotion she'd yet to channel into her art.

She traced a finger over a sketch of his shoulder, the one he'd twisted towards her as she'd asked. It was coming. She could feel it in her fingertips. A tingle like she'd brushed them over a bud on the point of bursting. Wrapped energy on the cusp of explosion.

Jed's cattle mooed in the background. Scarlett looked up, smiling. It must be milking time, which she supposed was what Sam would be doing now. Whatever that involved, she bet he was good at it.

She bet he was wonderful in bed, too.

'For God's sake.' Throwing her hands up, Scarlett leapt from the stool and paced the room. She circled once, twice, stopping on the third lap at a pile of paintings she'd attempted in the weeks after Christmas, when a combination of loneliness and frustration had had the black hole at its deepest. She gave the front frame a kick. It tumbled end over end before flopping on its back.

'Crap,' she said, quickly snatching it up and setting it canvas in to the wall. The last thing she needed was to see Felix's face, even if it was a distorted, stylised image of him. She'd made him ghoulish, ugly. A soot-black soul who didn't deserve redemption.

He did though. That was the worst of it. As painful as it was, and despite the scorch marks on her own soul, she couldn't bring herself to hate him.

More moos filtered in. Scarlett wondered what colour a dairy cow's soul would be. Shamrock green? Milky white?

She giggled and put her fingers to her forehead. Going mad, that's what she was doing. Completely and utterly bonkers.

She looked around the room, at her art, her life, then snatched up her keys and bag and headed out.

'You do realise,' said Audrey in tones as regal as her Egyptian-blue silk top, 'that isolating yourself the way you are does nothing to fill your creative well.'

Scarlett paused to sniff a rose but really to give herself time not to lose her temper. She'd thought a dose of reality from Audrey would help. Instead, she was on the end of a lecture about how to live a creative life. A bit rich coming from someone who wasn't an artist.

'I'm not locking myself away.'

Audrey took an elegant puff on her cigar and watched the smoke lazily dissipate in the late-afternoon air. Bar an occasional relieving zephyr, the atmosphere remained stubbornly thick and still, not helping Scarlett's fractiousness.

At least the fragrant smoke kept the bugs away, and there were plenty buzzing about Camrick's magnificent rose garden. The historic, two-storey mansion where Audrey lived with her daughter, Adrienne, and Adrienne's partner, Samuel, peered over them like a lacey old dowager, its bullnose verandah hooding its windows in a scowl as though it had witnessed more scenes like this than it cared for.

'Of course you're not,' said Audrey.

'Don't start. I'm not in the mood.'

Audrey studied her. 'Ah,' she said.

Scarlett tensed. She knew that tone too well. Experience had taught her not to bite, but curiosity won out. 'Ah what?'

'Your model. You like him.'

Scarlett answered with a roll of her eyes.

'You do.' Audrey waggled the cigar at her. 'And you don't know what to do with him.'

'I'm a red-blooded woman. I know exactly what to do with an attractive man, but I'm not trying to bed him. I'm trying to get my mojo back.'

'Perhaps one could lead to another. It has been a while since Felix.'

Nineteen months, to be exact. And every one of them a relief after the anxiety and malice that had infected the final, tumultuous weeks of their relationship.

Scarlett had to admit she did miss sex. No, not just sex. Sex and the other bits that came with it. *Intimacy*. Cuddles and soft murmurs, adoring kisses on the forehead, hand squeezes and quiet 'I love yous'.

'How do you know I haven't hooked up with anyone?'

Audrey eyed her up and down. 'If you were having regular sex, Scarlett, you wouldn't be quivering like a whippet at the thought.' She puffed several times, somehow making the act elegant instead of the filthy habit it was. 'It really is very good for you.'

'So are prunes, but as with everything there are consequences.'

Audrey let out an indecorous snort of laughter.

Scarlett smiled. Theirs was an unusual friendship but a valuable one.

'I do believe,' said Audrey, serious again, 'that getting out would help. You've had quite long enough to lick your wounds.' She held up her hand to stop Scarlett's protest. 'No, don't start. Yes, you were hurt and yes, Felix deserves to be strung up for what he did, but you're a talented and capable woman about to step into what I believe will be an extraordinary future. If,' she pointed the ashy end of her cigar at Scarlett, 'and only if, you take the opportunities coming to you.

'You're going to be living in close quarters with others in

London. Not only will mingling be expected, it will be vital for your career. You're experienced enough to know how cutthroat this business can be. Do not expect the industry to fall at your feet simply because you earned a prestigious award.' Cigar clenched between her teeth, Audrey deadheaded a spent rose. 'You might find it shameful, but a bit of sucking up never hurts.'

'I'm not totally socially inept, you know.'

'Perhaps not. However, you spend too much time alone and in your own head. Given your current state, that's far too fertile an environment for doubts to breed. Fear in an artist is good. If you're not feeling fear, you're not stretching yourself. Doubts, on the other hand, are dangerous and corrosive. Breed too many and they'll eat you from the inside out. As you've seen yourself.'

'If you're suggesting I'm turning into some sort of Felix—'

'Don't be ridiculous.' Though unfinished, Audrey tossed her cigar to the path and ground it out with the toe of her expensive loafer. 'All I'm suggesting is that you open yourself up. Let some fresh air into that clouded head of yours.'

'Sam is—'

'Sam?'

Scarlett sighed. She had hoped to keep Sam to herself. 'Sam Greenwood.'

Audrey's blue-sky gaze narrowed. Scarlett could see her mentally flicking through her index of Levenham locals, trying to place him. Finding him, she couldn't keep the glee out of her voice. 'Karen Patzel's son?'

'Yes.'

'How serendipitous.'

She supposed that was one word for it.

Audrey eyed her again. Scarlett folded her arms and used her toe to kick a stone from the garden bed back onto the carriageway. Only God knew what mischief was now forming inside that old brain.

'I don't believe I've met young Sam. When did you say he would be modelling again?'

'I didn't.'

'Don't be selfish, Scarlett.'

'You're not coming to perve on him.'

'Observe, not perve. What do you think I am?'

'Do you really want me to answer that?'

Audrey smiled and wandered to a new rose bush. 'Getting back to your problem, I am quite serious about this locking-yourself-away business. You are not doing yourself, or your creativity, any favours.'

'Perhaps not, but I don't see the point in developing a new social circle right now, either.'

'There is always a point in developing social connections. Although personally, I think a tumble with your model man would do the job just as well.'

'No. That is a complication I don't need.' No matter how appealing it sounded.

'Then you won't mind if I borrow him, will you?'

'You can try,' said Scarlett sweetly, 'but then I'll have to show him your nude sketches.' She dropped her voice. 'The unfortunate ones.'

'Cruel child.'

Smug with the hit she'd scored, Scarlett tucked her arm through Audrey's. 'Learned it from you, my old friend. Learned every trick from you.'

EIGHT

SAM ARRIVED EARLY on Wednesday afternoon bearing a bottle of his special Jersey milk, which Scarlett accepted with a mixture of bemusement and curiosity. How good could milk get? When she'd first moved in, Jed had offered to drop by containers of straight-out-of-the-cow fresh milk, but she'd refused, preferring skim milk from the supermarket in Levenham. It was what she was used to, and, truth be told, the thought of raw, unpasteurised milk made her slightly queasy.

Her thanks to Sam for his gift was to ask him to pose with his top removed. A request he was more than happy to comply with, given the speed at which he whipped off his Bells Beach Surf Classic–emblazoned t-shirt. And his self-satisfied smile.

It was another mucky hot day and the ceiling fans did little other than stir up enough breeze to half-dry the sweat greasing Scarlett's skin. Alone, she would have stripped down to her underwear or perhaps worked nude. With Sam she'd have to suffer.

Although gazing at his form involved no suffering at all.

His shoulders were magnificent. Swimmer's shoulders, straight, broad and muscled, and carving into equally beautiful arms. The kind that, when wrapped around a loved one, offered protection and the fuzzy, warm feeling that came from being held close and adored.

Scarlett found herself mesmerised by their lines. The stretch of his trapezius, the breadth of his latissimus dorsi. The angle of his scapular and dip of his collarbone. The bulge of his biceps and triceps. Muscle and bone names she'd learned long ago in life-drawing class and never thought she'd need to remember.

Shadows and light.

Power.

Her page quickly filled with partials. Her fingers had that tingle again, as though she was being led into the unknown and her job was to sketch her way out.

'Have you always surfed?' she asked after a while.

'Yeah. Dad used to take me out with him when I was little.'

'Your dad surfs too?'

'Not as much as he used to.'

'And your mum?'

'She boogieboards sometimes, but mostly she just swims.'

'You're a regular family of water babies.'

He broke his classical discus-thrower's pose to sweep his eyes over her, his gaze appreciative. Scarlett wished he wouldn't. She was having enough trouble as it was separating her creative interest from her sexual one. 'You're not a swimmer?'

'Not like you. I can swim, of course, but it's not something I do often. I burn.' She indicated the eggshell fragility of her alabaster skin.

'Wear a bodysuit. I'm sure my sisters would have one lying about somewhere that you could borrow. The ocean's good for you. Mum reckons she solves the world's problems in the water.'

'It's the negative ions.' Scarlett tutted at his scepticism. 'Don't laugh. They're great for creativity. It's the flow of water, the molecules separating and rejoining, releasing energy. A shower or bath can have the same effect.'

'I'm usually too busy trying to catch a wave to get creative.' He returned to his pose. Scarlett reminded herself to tell him to break soon. The discus pose was painful to maintain, even when not holding a weight. It was, however, delicious to look at. 'Or wishing Dylan would shut up. He's my mate. Runs a surfboard-making shop in Port Andrews. Or tries to. He surfs more than works. Can talk the hind leg off a horse. I think it's the resin he uses, does something to his brain. Good board-maker, though.'

'He sounds interesting.'

Sam's reply cracked back like a shot. 'Not that interesting.'

Scarlett bit her bottom lip to hide her smile.

'You should come to the beach with me one day,' said Sam after a while.

'Sam.'

'I'm not flirting. I'm looking out for your creativity.'

'My creativity is fine.' A lie, but she wasn't about to reveal her problem to Sam.

'Your education, then.'

'My education?'

'Yeah. Who knows when you'll be asked to do a portrait of a famous surfer?'

She laughed and regarded him. 'The only surfer I'm interested in is you.'

'Glad to hear it.'

Noting the strain in his voice, Scarlett told him to relax. As he shook the arm he'd had stretched out, she studied her drawings. Again, she experienced that frisson of being on the edge of discovery.

Still the edge, though. Not stepping off the cliff.

What would it take?

She sighed, flipped over the page and considered his next pose. Maybe something less strenuous. Something more him.

Scarlett fetched the simple fold-out chair from near her bed that she mostly threw half-worn clothes on, placed it in front of the easel and sat to demonstrate the pose she wanted.

'No worries,' said Sam, taking her spot. He rested forward, elbows on his thighs, hands clasped together and head up.

'Did you want anything to drink first? The discus pose can take it out of you.'

'I'm fine, and this is relaxing.'

He certainly looked relaxed. His smile easy, his forearms draped between his legs.

Scarlett drank some water and picked up her charcoal, feeling Sam's eyes following her every move. A shiver ran through her. Not cold. Awareness. As if they were exchanging energy, like ions.

'Tell me about your milk,' said Scarlett, as she drew her first lines.

'Pure Jersey milk. Best there is.'

'Why?'

'Higher butterfat content, mostly, but it also has a unique flavour from the pastures we graze our cattle on. Have you heard of the French wine term "terroir"?'

'I have.' It had been a favourite subject of Felix's, usually when he'd had too much. He liked to compare the art of a winemaker to that of a sculptor. How they were simply bettering what nature had already made. Once, that had been true for Felix, before bitterness corroded his talent and left acid holes in his imagination. Such a waste. For him and for her.

'My milk has it. It comes from our soils, the natural flora and fauna of the farm and its microclimate. We're close to the sea and wetlands, making our grazing conditions unique.'

'I thought milk was just milk.'

'Most people do because that's how most of it is sold—as a commodity. But dairy cattle produce different lactic bacteria in their milk, depending on where and what they're grazing. Our microclimate, our bacteria, are special, so our milk's special.'

'Call me a squeamish city girl, but I'm not sure I like the idea of bacteria in my milk.'

'Squeamish city girl.'

She laughed.

Sam grinned then turned serious. 'I've been drinking raw milk since I was born. Hasn't hurt me. Or my sisters or Jed, or any of Jed's kids. My sisters and I used to squirt warm milk from the teat straight into our mouths. Bloody beautiful. You should try it.'

'No thanks.'

He let out an exaggerated sigh.

'So the milk you sell is raw?'

'No, it's pasteurised. Has to be. It's illegal to sell raw milk for human consumption in Australia, which means that a lot of the flavour is lost, but it still retains enough small molecule flavour to give it terroir. I don't press home too much about that because that's not as good a marketing message as the milk's other qualities. Mostly, I focus on the milk's richness—its protein, fat and calcium content, and mouth feel. Jersey milk goes down like liquid velvet. It's also great for coffee. Baristas love it.'

'You make it sound magical.'

'It is.'

She paused to study him. Something had changed. Where relaxation and ease had been, now there was eagerness. The sense of wanting to rise, to pace while moving his hands, forming the shapes of his passion.

'The cusp,' she said softly.

Sam tilted his head. 'The cusp?'

'Oh, nothing.' She drew a few lines. It was coming. Slowly—too slowly—but coming. All she had to do was be aware and responsive enough to capture it.

She had Sam change poses several more times, hunting for the trigger that would fill her head with ideas. As with the previous session, it remained out of reach.

'Thanks, Sam,' she said at the end of their time. Though she tried to sound upbeat, it was hard to keep the failure out of her voice.

'It's not working?' he asked, threading his arms into the sleeves of his shirt, then hooking his thumbs in the neck and pulling the fabric over his head in one fluid movement.

Scarlett watched the ripple of his chest and belly as his muscles clenched. No six-pack, gym-junkie here. Just a toned, healthy man who farmed for a living and surfed for recreation. A man whose belly she'd like to run her tongue over.

She pressed her hand to her forehead. It was the heat. It had to be the heat. 'Not how I'd like.'

'Come for a swim. I'll be finished milking by six. We

can have a swim and eat fish and chips on the beach after. Or a burger. Or you could go all out and have roast chicken and coleslaw. It's gourmet all the way, down at Port Andrews.'

Scarlett thought of Audrey's admonition about shutting herself away. What Sam was proposing wasn't socialising, though. It sounded romantic, like first-date silly stuff that made her heart squeeze with yearning. It had been years since she'd done anything romantic. Felix had stopped trying a long time ago. As had she.

Except what point was there in doing it now?

'Maybe another day.'

His sparkling eyes held hers. 'I'll hold you to that.'

'We'll see.' Deliberately, she turned from that lovely gaze and rattled through her tray. 'I'll see you on Sunday.'

'Sure thing.'

Footsteps faded towards the door. Scarlett kept her head down.

'Scarlett?'

She regarded him.

'Try my milk.'

'I will.'

As soon as she heard his car start, Scarlett regretted her refusal. A swim might clear her head of the cobwebs that had formed there. And swimming with Sam would give her the opportunity to see him in an environment he clearly loved.

She threw down the piece of charcoal, not caring that it snapped on landing. She had the urge to kick and slash again. For a few heartbeats, she considered giving Felix's portrait the 'Psycho-Enter Sandman' treatment and decided that was too good for him. The only thing he deserved was fire. Except Levenham was under a total fire ban, where even lighting a barbecue was illegal. Nor was Scarlett sure it would be cathartic like her mini-slasher-fest. Burning art, even ugly art, skidded too close to the scars on her soul.

Instead, she paced, until she finally paused at her wardrobe. A forest-green bikini was tucked at the back of her underwear drawer. She tugged it out and held up the slinky triangles that made up the top.

The last time she'd worn it was seared on her brain. A pool party at Felix's friend's place in the expensive suburb of Unley Park. Scarlett hadn't wanted to go. It had had danger written all over it, but Felix had insisted. The young creative set were out in packs. Fine art students budding with dreams, some with real talent, eager to mix with established and up-and-coming artists like Scarlett in the hope that some of her success would rub off.

She'd responded politely to the students while watching Felix with wary eyes. He was fine at first, then the drinks had started going down too well and he'd begun to stalk like the cat of his name, mouth twitching and claws out. Scarlett had taken his arm, urging him home. He'd jerked out of her grip, a snarl lifting his mouth.

Partygoers had stared. Amusement had fluttered. The glamour couple were having a tiff, how funny.

Except it hadn't been a tiff and it had been a lifetime from funny.

Scarlett shoved the bikini back in the drawer and slammed it shut.

Not a memory for today. Not a memory for any time.

The ocean could wait.

NINE

IT WAS ONLY a matter of time before Sam bumped into Jed. The surprise was that it had taken this long for Jed to manufacture what Sam suspected was an accidentally on purpose meeting. Not that he minded. Sam had nothing to hide.

And Jed wasn't exactly 'perfect man' competition.

The thought left Sam smiling as he veered to one side of the potholed track and pulled up, Jed doing the same. Their windows met, driver to driver, side mirrors nearly touching in the easy dance of many a country meeting.

Sam lowered his window. The heatwave had given over to a milder summer's day of clear skies tempered by a cooling breeze scented with the distinct aroma of a working dairy farm. 'Jed, how's things?'

'Not bad. You?'

'Can't complain. Faye good?'

'Yep, yep. Keeping busy with her craft work. Your mum and dad?'

'They're great. Mum's working too much, as usual.

Dad's making noises again about the retirement he'll probably never get around to.'

'Your old man'll be like me. Still pulling teats when he should be fishing.' Jed scratched at his cheek where a large red spot stood out from his tanned wrinkles. 'Or whatever it is that retirees do. Milk prices what they are, I've a mind to discover it myself.'

Sam would believe that when he saw it. Jed wouldn't have invested so heavily in his new dairy if he hadn't planned on staying in the industry.

'Nasty-looking bite there.'

'March fly. Didn't notice the bugger until it'd sunk its teeth in.' Big, ugly and clumsy, march flies were a common summer pest, especially along the coast, and considered anything warm-blooded fair game. Sam had endured his fair share of painful bites over the years. Jed scratched some more and dropped his hand with a sigh and eyed him. 'You here to see young Scarlett?'

'I am.'

Jed nodded again, his lips pursing in and out. 'Modelling, are you?'

Sam blinked. 'How did you know?'

'Did a bit myself. Hard work it is, too.' He chuckled. 'Never would have believed it.'

Whether Jed was expressing disbelief over his own modelling or how hard it was, Sam wasn't sure. He was still trying to cope with the shock that Jed had modelled at all. So much for Sam thinking he was the only perfect model.

A cog in his thickened brain clicked over, dragging a horrible thought with it. Had Jed been nude?

'Did some nice drawings, too,' said Jed, unaware of Sam's shock. 'Faye was right impressed.' He nodded, as if agreeing with himself. 'Talented girl.'

'She sure is.'

Jed's nose screwed up a fraction. 'Bit strange, though, don't you reckon?'

'What makes you ask that?'

'Oh, nothin'. Just a few odd things that got me thinking a bit.'

Sam was curious now. 'Like what?'

Jed lifted his hand off the steering wheel. 'Ack, forget I said anything. Not right to gossip about tenants.'

'No, I suppose not.' Except Sam was itching to push for more. Scarlett had been fine since their first meeting, if he didn't count the weird mutterings about 'cusps' or the defeat in her voice and posture when he went to leave on Wednesday. The former he figured was just some artist's affectation. The latter had bothered him. She didn't seem the type to give in to defeat.

He focused on the old dairy, wondering if she was observing the encounter. The shutters were tilted open, but there was no movement behind them that Sam could see.

'She's been a good one, too,' said Jed. 'Tenant, I mean.'

'That's handy.'

'Shame she's leaving.'

Sam's focus snapped back to Jed. 'Leaving?'

'Uh-huh. End of March. Won some six-month-long painting scholarship to London.'

Sam could have sworn Jed's chest puffed out as he spoke. Meanwhile, his felt like it was caving in.

Scarlett was leaving. Not just Levenham, but the country, and she hadn't said a word.

Why should she, though? As far as she was concerned, their relationship was professional. Mutual attraction didn't mean they had anything deeper. They didn't owe each other anything.

'Right,' said Sam for no other reason than he couldn't think of anything else to say.

'Ah, well. This isn't getting any work done. Good to see you, Sam. Say g'day to your mum and dad for me.'

'Will do. Give Faye my best.'

Jed's ute bumped off. Sam's stayed where it was.

It was stupid to feel betrayed, yet he did. And not because he'd pulled on his best trunks in case Scarlett wanted him to pose with more than his top off, or that he'd planned to invite her to the launch of Kai's autumn menu—an exclusive event for suppliers and selected customers to be held Monday week. The invitation had arrived a few weeks ago and Sam hadn't thought much of it at the time, except that he'd go. Now he figured it was the perfect date-without-being-a-date. Provided she said yes.

He felt betrayed because he'd finally met a gorgeous, intriguing girl whom he'd like to know better, only for her to be on the verge of skipping town.

Talk about the universe kicking him in the nuts.

Just as well Sam was the positive type or he'd be a bit miserable about the whole thing. Not to worry, Scarlett wasn't gone yet. He still had time to work some Greenwood charm, and six months wasn't long to wait for the right girl.

And his gut—along with other bits—was telling him that Scarlett was very right.

'Hey,' he said, when she opened the door.

'Hey, you. Thanks for coming.'

'No problem.' Sam stepped inside, catching a whiff of paint and something else chemical as he passed. To his surprise, the easel held a canvas instead of her usual sketch-book. A trolley table stood alongside, laden with tubes and brush pots and messy with paint. 'You've been painting.'

'Sort of.' She shut the door, strode to the easel and began to lift off the canvas.

'Can I see?' asked Sam.

Scarlett hesitated then set the painting down. Indicating for him to go ahead, she stepped back and wrapped one arm across her breasts, her fingers toying with her bottom lip. Odd behaviour, given she'd never been shy about her work before, even with her erotic pictures.

Sam scanned the painting. It was some sort of abstract piece concocted of cartoon-pig-pink limbs on a kaleidoscope background of blues and greens. There were two oversized arms, maybe a leg, quite possibly a penis, though it could have been another leg, and a giant sludge-coloured eye. As for the rest, he had no idea.

'It's colourful,' he said carefully. Which it was.

Unease crept up his spine as he contemplated the eye thing again. Despite the style, it was quite realistic, its wet paint glistening as if the eye had just blinked. The iris was browny-green with fiery flecks of orange and gold, reminiscent of how his own appeared in the right light.

The unease worsened. Was this meant to be him? Shit, he hoped not. That would be seriously unflattering.

'I suppose that's one word for it.' With a grimace, Scarlett lifted the painting off the easel and carried it to the wall, where she dumped the canvas face in, apparently unconcerned that the work was still wet, and stood with her hands on her hips, scowling at it.

'Bad day?'

'Just a bit.' She huffed out a breath and gave him a strained smile. 'But you're here to make it better.' She waved at the chair, already in position. 'Ready? Or would you prefer a drink first?'

'I'm fine.' Sam went to sit down and stopped. 'Shirt on or off?'

Scarlett made a dismissive gesture as if she didn't care either way. 'Oh, off, I suppose.'

He frowned and peeled off his polo shirt, wondering what was up. Sam knew what was wrong with him, but Scarlett was acting as odd as her painting. Hoping for at least a smile, he twirled his shirt like a stripper and flung it towards the kitchen table. To no reaction. Scarlett's attention remained elsewhere.

Huh. Well, that put him in his place.

The paint trolley had been replaced with the smaller table that held her sketching paraphernalia. Scarlett picked up a piece of charcoal, inspected it, then swapped it for another before putting that down and plucking up a ball of putty rubber. She stared at the blank sheet of her sketchpad, kneading the eraser and chewing her bottom lip.

It was as though she'd forgotten Sam was there. Another dent to his ego. Not that his ego couldn't take a few hits. Sam had enough self-confidence to cope with being both ignored and portrayed as a Picasso-style pig. He wasn't so sure about Scarlett.

She looked tired. Her pale skin was almost translucent, the area under her eyes tinged a faint blue. Her braided hair had come loose and tendrils stuck to her damp neck. There was paint on her arms and on her singlet and cargo pants, and her skin had the greasy sheen of someone who'd been toiling hard. Even more troubling was her posture. Not hunched, more a protective curl. Only slight, but by now Sam was attuned to her normal working posture and this wasn't it.

'Are you okay?'

She looked up. 'Sorry?'

He smiled. 'I asked if you were okay.'

'Oh.' She set the putty rubber down, then, as though suddenly aware of her appearance, smoothed hair back from her forehead and tucked away the tendrils. 'I'm fine. Busy, that's all.'

'Busy' Sam believed. 'Fine' he didn't. Except they weren't close enough yet for him to feel comfortable digging further. Maybe after, if he could get her talking. And perhaps thinking of him as human instead of a disembodied bunch of pink limbs.

'How do you want me to pose?' he asked.

Scarlett settled her gaze on him, tilted her head to the side and screwed up her nose. 'Would you be okay with taking your shorts off?'

'No problem.'

He had them off in moments.

'Can you ...' She tapped a finger against her chin, focus lingering on his legs. Then her shoulders sagged and she rubbed her brow, her voice coming on a tired-sounding sigh. 'Just stand normally.'

He regarded his legs. 'Are they that bad?' He lifted one up and twisted it back and forth. 'I thought they were handsome legs. Good thighs.' He gave the top a bit of a thump. 'Solid.'

'They're very good legs.'

'That's all right, then. I was getting worried.' When that still didn't earn a reaction he added, 'Are you sure you're okay?'

'Yes, of course.' She managed a faint smile. 'A bit of a headache, but nothing serious.'

'I have some tablets in the ute, if you need some.'

'Thanks, but it'll pass. Most likely I haven't drunk enough water. I tend to forget to hydrate when I'm working.

Anyway, enough of that.' She clapped her hands together. 'Let's try something more you. How do you stand when you surf?'

Sam placed one foot forward, the other back, and crouched a little to lower his centre of gravity, his front arm up. 'Like this, I suppose.'

'That's perfect. Can you hold it?'

'Sure.'

She picked up a stick of charcoal and after a moment's pause began to sketch.

'Did you try my milk?' Sam asked after a while, both out of curiosity and because he needed something to distract him from the effort of holding his stance.

'I did.'

'And?'

'You were right. It tasted different.'

'I'm hoping not in a bad way.'

'No. Not in a bad way.' Scarlett made a series of short strokes. 'I can see why it's in demand, though. I've never tasted milk so creamy.'

'Told you.' He drew in a breath. 'Speaking of being in demand, Kai—he's the chef at Restaurant Ten—is holding a suppliers' night Monday week. It's his way of saying thanks and to show off some of his upcoming autumn menu. My invitation is for two. Would you like to come?'

Scarlett seemed to pause, hovering the charcoal over the pad. 'It's a nice invitation ...'

'It's not a date. I just thought it'd be a fun night out. And it'd save me the embarrassment of turning up alone.'

'Alone? I hardly think that would be a problem. I bet you have plenty of women who'd jump at the chance to be your date.'

'Good of you to think so, but no, I don't.'

The look she shot him was pure 'spare me'. 'I find that very hard to believe.'

He laughed. 'It's true. Ask around.'

'Oh, come on, Sam. Look at you.' She waved the charcoal as though outlining his body. 'You're attractive, fit. You run your own business—successfully by all appearances—and you're smart, with an engineering degree no less. What's not to like?' Her expression narrowed. 'Unless you're hiding some horrible personality disorder.'

'Not that I'm aware of, although my sisters might beg to differ. Nah, it's not that. It's the dairy-farming bit. It's not for everyone.'

'Neither is the uncertainty of being with an artist, but relationships are about give and take. That's what makes them work.'

He shrugged. 'That's what I always believed too, but I guess there's just more take in dairying.' At her arched eyebrow, he went on. 'It's day in, day out. A life commitment as well as a business, which doesn't leave a lot of room for spontaneity. For some, the grind can be a disappointment.'

'The voice of experience?'

Talking about past relationships was never a good idea in Sam's book, but he was the idiot who'd brought up the subject.

'Yeah.'

She was quiet for a moment, the charcoal spinning as she rotated it between her fingers, her eyes locked on his. 'What happened?'

'Not much. She just decided she didn't want that kind of life.'

Scarlett leaned forward slightly and regarded him with her head tilted, and for the first time since his arrival, Sam

felt she was really seeing him. 'Surely your girlfriend understood your passion for dairying and the life it entailed when
you started going out?'

'She did, in theory. But I guess it's like a lot of things,
you don't really understand until you live it.' He shrugged
again, hiding the hurt that still lingered a little. Cassie was a
great girl. They'd had a lot of fun and some days, when he
was feeling sorry for himself because things weren't going
right or he had come home to an empty, cold house, Sam
wished her back in his life. That wouldn't happen, though.
He didn't want it and neither did she.

'How long were you together?'

'Three years. Lived together for nearly a year.'

Sympathy gentled her gaze. 'That's a long time.'

It was. Sam had thought it was going to last, too and had
contemplated popping the question more than once. Some
gut instinct had held him back. Good thing he'd listened
to it.

'Better we worked it out when we did. It could have
been a hell of a lot worse.'

'Yes.' Scarlett's focus drifted to her rows of paintings
and her tone lowered further. 'Breakups can be ugly.'

'Now who's talking like the experienced one?'

She smiled sadly. 'We all have our histories, Sam.'

From the way she said it, Scarlett's had left scars. Deep
ones. Which might explain why she'd needed the services
of his mum, who specialised in family law. When Sam had
asked, his mum had simply patted his head and told him he
was a big enough boy to find these things out for himself.

'I guess we're both battle-worn,' said Sam, with deliberate cheer. They needed to get off this topic. 'Good thing
ruggedness becomes me.'

'Battle-worn?' Scarlett chuckled and Sam was relieved

at the change. He didn't like her sounding sad or defeated. He liked her bright, like her art. He even liked her when she was being weird. 'You,' she said, picking up her charcoal and pointing it at him, 'can be battle-worn. I prefer to think of myself as older and wiser. Now ...' She flipped the sketchpad over to a clean page. 'This older and wiser person suggests we work.'

TEN

IT TOOK a while for Sam to realise that Scarlett had side-stepped his invitation to Kai's party. He decided not to push. Asking again while standing in trunks, even trendy new ones, wouldn't do his cause any good. The discus pose was uncomfortable, but at least it felt athletic and cool, like a classical sculpture. The fake surfer one just felt stupid.

'These look great,' said Sam when Scarlett called for him to take a break and he inspected her work. No sign of pink legs or penises or whatever they were now. Thank God.

'They're okay.'

He glanced at her. 'You're not convinced?'

'I'm not. I mean I am.' She rubbed her forehead. 'It's hard to explain.'

'Try me.'

'They're just images.'

'Good ones, from what I can tell.'

As with her other sketches, she'd captured him not photo-realistically but in a way that still showed himself. There were lines everywhere. Some were short, thick and dark, suggesting strength. Others trailed like wisps, reminding him of half-dissolved jet streams in the sky. For something two-dimensional, the sketches displayed astonishing energy and animation, as though Sam was about to surf into the room on white waves of paper.

'Good doesn't make great art, unfortunately.'

'Okay.' Clearly, he was missing something. 'What does, then?'

Scarlett dragged both hands down her face, smudging her cheeks with charcoal. 'I wish I knew.' She took a sharp breath. 'I'm sorry, Sam. You don't need to be hearing this. Grab yourself a drink. I'll be back in a tick.'

She hurried to the bathroom. Sam remained where he was, hands on his hips and alternating between eyeing the space separating them and Scarlett's sketchpad. Splashing water echoed from the open bathroom door. A few minutes later she emerged, clean-cheeked and with droplets of water spangling her dark hair.

'That's better,' she said. 'Have you had a drink?'

'No. How about we both have one?' Sam didn't wait for her to answer. He fetched glasses from the shelf and cold water from the fridge, noting how much was missing from his milk bottle. Half. Not bad, and a positive indicator that she hadn't lied about trying it.

Scarlett accepted the glass with a smile that didn't fool Sam for a second. She was upset about something and he wanted to know what it was.

'Want to share the problem?' he asked. 'I might not know anything about art, but I'm a good listener.'

'That's sweet of you, but it's very boring.'

'Nothing about you is boring.'

She gave him one of her looks over the rim of her glass. 'Sam.'

'It's the truth.' He took a mouthful of water. 'Is it the scholarship?'

She lowered the glass and stared into it for a few heartbeats before looking up. 'I guess that means you've heard.'

'Yeah, Jed told me.'

'It's not a scholarship. It's a six-month residency for fine artists and an incredible honour. Only four people are chosen each year and I was lucky enough to be one of them.'

Sam doubted luck had much to do with it. Even he could appreciate Scarlett's talent. 'So, you just go over there and paint for six months?'

'Yes and no. The painting part is important, but the other purpose of the residency is for the chosen artist to develop artistically and professionally through building relationships with other artists and industry. The building itself is like a commune, with studios and recreation rooms, and there are staff on hand to assist with research, introductions, gallery visits, you name it.'

'Sounds like an amazing opportunity.'

'It is. Or it would be if I could still paint.'

Sam couldn't help his glance at her lined-up canvases.

'Most of them are rubbish,' she said. 'I lost my creativity with a painting called *Crowns* and now I can't get it back.'

'But you thought you could with me?'

'Yes. The perfect man.' She smiled wanly. 'I had the idea that if I created a masculine series to counter my feminine one, it would give me my mojo back.'

'And it's not working. Despite my perfect man-ness.'

'Not like I hoped, no. And not because your man-ness isn't perfect. It is. It's me.'

'The old it's me not you, huh?'

Scarlett gave a half-laugh and for a moment the

shadows edged away. Then her gaze returned to her sketchpad and her sweet cupid's bow mouth flattened.

'Okay,' said Sam. 'What can I do to help?'

She spread her fingers. 'I wish I knew.'

Sam wished he knew too. This was beyond his experience. He gazed around the space, thinking. It would be easy to dismiss her concerns—the rows of artworks belied her words, demonstrating she hadn't completely lost her creativity—but he had enough respect for Scarlett's talent to believe her when she said they weren't up to scratch.

She touched his arm. 'It's not your problem, Sam.'

'I know, but I'm a helpful kind of guy, and I have a "perfect man" reputation to uphold. Besides, I help you with this, maybe you'll agree to be my date for Kai's party.'

'If you can help me with this, then I'll be your date for anything you like.'

'You're on. First up,' he said, plucking the glass from her grip with one hand and tangling the other with hers, 'let's get out of here.'

Sam drove her to the farm.

Scarlett had protested at first, demanding to take her own car, but Sam refused, even though it would mean a round trip. The whole idea was for her to clear her head and do something surprising and different and maybe inspirational. Trundling along in his ute would help that.

Or not. He had no idea. Whatever the outcome, it had to be better than leaving her alone in her studio with all those failed works lined up like teeth ready to bite.

It was a gorgeous day, the kind where showing off the land you loved came easy. Sam took his time, choosing detours and pointing out landmarks—Albert's Sinkhole, one of many in the area, and a popular haunt for cave divers; the paddock where he and Davey Buckman had rolled an old

Ford while doing circle work when they were fourteen, totalling the car and earning them both clips under the ear from their parents; the clifftop carpark where he experienced his first kiss; his favourite surf beach.

The stories brought smiles to Scarlett's face. She asked questions, too, about the landscape, the farms and their histories, the animals and people he knew.

'It's beautiful country,' she said, when they'd passed through the seaside village of Port Andrews and were on the windy, coast-hugging road to Heatherbrae.

'It is.'

'You love it, don't you?'

'Yeah, I do. It's why I came back, I suppose.' He rubbed his jaw. The surf was up. With a bit of luck, he'd get out on it this afternoon. 'I feel happy here. Free.' He shrugged, feeling embarrassed. Such a dumb thing to say, that you felt free. Freedom was a state of mind, not a place. 'Free's not the right word. Relaxed is probably more accurate. Except when the bottling plant breaks down. That's not very relaxing.'

'It's because you're doing something you love and are good at.'

'Yeah. Maybe.'

'There's a lot to be said for living what you love. Many people don't, and they live half-lives, not quite happy, not satisfied, either.'

There was truth in that. Sam had mates who fitted that description, always saying how one day they'd change things, live the life they'd fantasised about as a teenager, follow their dreams instead of slogging away at a job or business or even a relationship because that was what convention and expectation dictated. But one day never seemed to come. Excuses got in the way—jobs, kids, debt, families—

every one of them valid and every one of them feeling like another drag on their dreams.

Sam didn't know what the answer was, only that he was glad of his choices and even more grateful for his happiness. 'I guess we're the fortunate ones, then.'

'I guess we are.'

They shared a smile that charged the small space between them with ... Sam didn't know. Recognition? Affinity? Whatever it was, it felt good. He concentrated on the road. Anything to stop from touching her.

He parked his car in the crushed limestone lane leading towards Heatherbrae's dairy and led Scarlett through a small paddock to a shed a short distance away. The shed was nothing special—a steepled, corrugated iron roof over corrugated iron walls, and ends with full-width sliding doors, both left open to let in light and fresh air—but it was as important to the farm's production as anything else.

'Is this your dairy?' asked Scarlett, poking the brim of her hat back where it had fallen over her eyes. Sam hadn't given her time to grab her own hat and she was wearing one of his—a too-large broad-brimmed straw Panama that had seen better days. She hadn't complained. Under the pounding sun, a tatty hat was better than none.

'No. Our dairy's in that shed.' Sam indicated the larger building with attached silos. In the distance, the dairy herd relaxed under a small stand of trees planted years before to provide shade in the summer and shelter in the winter. In a few hours, urged on by their full udders and the prospect of tasty hard feed, the cattle would rouse and begin to shuffle their way to the shed, their running order determined by their personalities—some bustling bullies, some shy dawdlers, others easygoing followers. Bovine schoolkids, heading to class.

A timber fence formed a yard at the front of the shed they were headed for. Sam opened a gate and ushered Scarlett through. 'This is much more fun than a dairy.'

He stopped at the entrance, watching her closely as her eyes adjusted to the shade and she could properly absorb the shed's interior.

Metal rail and wide-mesh pens filled with bark chips ran down either wall. Peeking at them from behind the mesh were calves. Big-eyed, big-eared and gangly. Some black and white, some tan, each with a bright-yellow, numbered ear tag and every one of them looking as adorable as a cuddly toy.

'Oh,' exclaimed Scarlett, her hands rushing to her mouth. Her green eyes were huge with delight and Sam was sure he spotted a quiver. She looked at him in wonder. 'Can I pat them?'

'Sure.'

He headed for the pen holding the most recently born Jersey calves. They bunched up, uncertain and eager at the same time. The strange big man usually meant milk and to a calf nothing was more exciting.

He caught one with ease and held it between his legs. 'Come on. She won't bite. She might suck you to death, though.'

Scarlett stroked the calf's head, then, feeling bolder, knelt in front of her to inspect her face. She cooed and petted, her pale, drawn face suddenly flushed with happiness. 'Aren't you the loveliest thing, oh yes you are.'

'Didn't Jed show you his calves when you moved in?' Showing off calves was a dairyman standard. Sam doubted Jed would have been able to help himself, especially with someone as pretty as Scarlett.

She looked up, her smile radiant and making Sam's

heart feel a million times too big for his chest. 'He did, but something like this never gets old. And your little Jerseys are like toy cows.' She blew the calf a kiss that Sam wished was for him. 'Isn't that right, sweetheart? You're just the cutest baby ever.'

The calf rewarded Scarlett's praise by snatching at her fingers and sucking hard. Scarlett's mouth made an 'O' before broadening into an enormous smile.

Sam breathed in deeply. He'd known the calves would lift Scarlett's spirits, but he hadn't expected her reaction to them to ratchet up his own feelings so hard. His head was giddy, his senses twanging like overstretched wire. If a heart could melt, his would be a puddle in his boots right now.

He took another long breath. The air smelled of wood-chips, milk and happiness. And Scarlett. Stunning, rose-cheeked Scarlett.

Oh, man. He was such a goner.

ELEVEN

SCARLETT STARED at the calendar pinned on the side of the fridge. Today was February 28th, which left three and a half weeks until she headed for Adelaide to finalise any remaining arrangements, and to spend a week with her mum before flying out. Twenty-five days to get her mojo back.

Twenty-five days to spend with Sam.

She butted her head against the calendar and squeezed her eyes shut. She should not be thinking about Sam in this way. He was her model, the 'perfect man' to haul her out of her black hole of creative nothingness. He would not—*could not*—be anything more.

For both their sakes.

Scarlett sighed and opened the fridge door. The bottle of Sam's Dairy Pure Jersey Milk was almost empty. Scarlett wasn't a big drinker of straight milk, but Sam was right about it being delicious, and now that she'd had a quick tour of his mini-factory and she'd seen the processes and hygiene involved, she felt much better about drinking it. She unscrewed the plastic lid and guzzled the last mouthfuls straight from the bottle, then grinned at her naughtiness.

'The joys of living alone,' she said aloud, wiping her mouth. She checked the bottle's base for a recycling symbol —of course it had one; she wouldn't expect otherwise from Sam—and left it on the bench to take to the recycling bin later.

Thirst quenched, Scarlett returned to her easel. The sketchpad was busy with drawings. Scarlett wasn't yet where she wanted to be, but since her trip to Heatherbrae she'd felt a hum inside her. The return of her creativity was close, very close. She could feel it trembling, like a burrowed animal sniffing the air, waiting for a safe moment to scamper out into the world.

It was nearly three days since her visit and her confidence that she'd recover from this setback was higher than it had been in weeks. Perhaps all she'd needed was a change of scenery. Perhaps it was Sam.

Seeing him in his home environment had stirred something inside her. He'd looked even more masculine than usual, more alive. His passion for dairying, for his herd, his growing business, the farm, was like an aura. He crackled with life. His lovely swimmer's shoulders were straighter than normal, his gorgeous gold-flecked eyes aglow. A smile kept lifting his mouth, and while she wouldn't call his walk a swagger—Sam was too laidback for that—it was the walk of a man comfortable in his skin and content with the life he'd made.

It was just as well she'd snatched up her phone before Sam had dragged her to the farm or she wouldn't have been able to photograph him and would have had to work from memory. She'd snapped him with the calves, in his bottling room, in the pit of the farm's herringbone dairy, walking to his ute.

The photos were now on her laptop, and she'd spent most of the morning working steadily through them, taking inspiration, willing his life force into her hands. Smiling back at his handsome, happy face. The drawings still weren't right, though. They still lacked that *je ne sais quoi* that turned her insides quivering with excitement and her fingers twitching with the urge to take her art to another level. To create a work that was more than an image. A work that sang, that connected. That made the viewer feel like they were being told the most marvellous of stories through colour and form.

Scarlett growled her frustration. She didn't have time to waste on angst or bad art. Whatever was lacking, she needed to fill the void, and soon. Other than driving to Heatherbrae for another dose of calf cuteness, the only way through was to work and hope that Sam's spark would ignite a flame. Besides, in a few hours Sam would arrive for his Wednesday sitting.

The thought shouldn't have made her heart tumble-turn, but it did.

'Did you always paint the way you do now?' Sam asked.

Scarlett glanced at him and back to her drawing. He was stripped down to a pair of trunks and posed like a captain staring out to sea, wary of approaching danger— head up, fists curled, body leaned slightly forward. With his messy, salt-wrecked hair, he looked more like a pirate than a captain. Either way, it was a seductive look.

She added a few more lines, teeth gritted with irritation. Not with Sam, with herself. She was so close. So. Damn. Close. He looked manly and hot, and made her pulse quicken—the right ingredients for inspiration. Why wouldn't it come?

'If you mean my process, then yes. Since university, at least. I always start with a lot of charcoal sketches, and then, when I know I have the right perspective, the right ...' She made a growly noise. 'I don't know. It's just a feeling I get. It's like ... I don't know how to explain it.'

'Try me.'

She sat back and puffed out her cheeks. 'When things are going well, when I'm really creative, it's like my mind fills with colours and shapes and movement, and I can't get them out onto the canvas quick enough.'

He regarded her with interest. 'Like a movie?'

'Kind of. Although not with a normal narrative. It's like I'm seeing a story, but it's a hidden story. One the viewer has to tell themselves.' She smiled apologetically. 'I'm not making much sense, I know. It's just so hard to explain.'

'Sounds sensible enough to me, even if it's not something I've experienced.' He indicated his head. 'Boring engineer's brain. Not a lot of visualisation going on. All numbers and words and left stuff. What are you seeing now?'

'Snatches of a story. It's like, I don't know, a television screen, but one where pixels have broken apart. They're lost, floating around in my head, trying to join. I can feel them wanting to connect. Their attraction. Except right now they can't fit. They're like a jigsaw puzzle that's been made wrong. God,' she said, rubbing her forehead. Despite his understanding, she still felt silly trying to explain. 'I must sound crazy.'

'A bit.' Sam softened his reply with a smile. 'It's interesting, though. I see engineering problems a bit like that. Like pieces of physics that I need to connect, except without the story or colour.' He tipped his chin towards the stacked paintings. 'The one you were doing on Sunday. Was that what you were trying to reproduce? The pixel jigsaw?'

'No. That was an experiment. A failed attempt to force the process.' Scarlett sighed and looked at her sketchbook, her mouth turning down as she regarded her work. 'And it simply refuses to be forced.'

'You'll get there. You just need something, or *someone*,' Sam grinned naughtily, 'to ignite it.'

'Someone like my model man, perhaps?'

He puffed out his chest even further. 'Your perfect model man, I'll have you know.'

Scarlett laughed. Sam was cute. If it weren't for him, she'd probably have succumbed to panic by now, but he had a way of making her feel that relief was close.

He also had a way of making her want to flirt back.

She put on her best stern-mother voice. 'My perfect model man needs to get back to his pose.'

Sam made a sweeping bow. 'I am at your service.'

'I actually wasn't asking about your process,' said Sam when they broke for a drink a little while later. He was leaned against the kitchen bench, watching her over the rim of his glass as she made tea for herself. 'I meant what you paint. The theme.'

'Oh.' She considered a moment. The kettle boiled and clicked off. She poured water into her mug, still thinking. 'Ongoing themes are a more recent happening. I used to do individual works, a lot of portraits, that kind of thing. Then I had this idea to do a series of paintings celebrating the feminine—its power and beauty. I was so enamoured with the idea, at the myriad perspectives, that I couldn't seem to stop painting them. They just kept coming. Like a ...' She waved a circle. 'A waterfall of creativity that seemed to come from nowhere, as if I was channelling them. It was amazing, like nothing I've ever experienced. There are over sixty paintings in that series. Your mum has one and you've seen some of the others. They sold well, too. Collectors snapped them up and I had a lot of people asking for more. I had plans to continue it, but ...' The excitement fell out of her voice. 'The waterfall dried up.'

'But always people? You don't do landscapes, that kind of thing?'

'No. I mean, I have. I've painted most subjects and tried all different kinds of styles. Landscapes, watercolours, pastels, portraits, abstracts. I did a lot of experimenting, especially at uni, but kept drifting back to people. They're interesting. You can reveal so much more about a person in a painting than you can in a photograph. A photographer would probably dispute that, but I think it's the truth.'

Sam smiled. 'I'd back you in a fight.'

'Thanks.' She returned his smile, wishing he would stop being so interested in her, and nice. Loving every moment of it.

'Have your paintings always sold?'

'God no.' She bobbed her teabag up and down. 'Some of my early stuff was terrible.'

'I bet it wasn't.'

'Believe me, it was. It wasn't until I found my creative voice that things started to take off. There were many lean years.' She tossed the teabag into the bin and added a splash of milk from the fresh bottle Sam had brought, and blew over the tea to cool it before taking a sip.

'What changed that?'

Scarlett knew where he was leading her. Sam was hunting for a trigger, the 'thing' that would switch her back on. She'd dug enough inside herself to know the answer wasn't in the past, but it was sweet of him to try. 'It was nothing sudden. Maturity, in a lot of ways. The more I worked the more confidence I gained. I had a few small successful exhibitions and it built from there. I was already primed, so to speak, when I had my feminine epiphany.'

'But you always believed in yourself?'

'Yes.' That was something Felix could never take away, though he'd tried. Little digs about being derivative, a poor man's version of multi-prize-winning artist Del Kathryn Barton. A throwaway comment about a work lacking surprise or authentic expression. The more his own talent had atrophied, the more savage he had become. And the more her own work had glittered.

'I like that. It's sexy.'

'Sam.'

'Yeah, I know.' There was zero repentance in his grin. 'Okay, so what's the work you're most proud of?'

'A trilogy of paintings called *My Own Eyes*.'

'Sounds intriguing.'

Scarlett could tell from his voice that he thought it was a self-portrait, probably a nude. They were nudes; however, not like he was imagining.

'My girlfriend Larissa had a baby—an adorable little cherub of a child with pudgy hands, the smile of a saint, and skin like nothing you've ever touched before. He was so gorgeous, so full of potential. I kept thinking, what will he become?'

'Everyone wonders that about babies, I suppose.'

'I never really had before. I think it was because he was Larissa's that I felt that way. What interested me even more was how besotted by each other mother and child were. It was extraordinary, the way they looked at one another. The more I saw it the more urgent my need to capture it became.'

'Clearly you did.'

'I did.' She shook her head, remembering. The miracle of those paintings would stay with her forever. 'Their bond was so intense it was almost otherworldly. It was after that I began my feminine series. I became intrigued with the power of womanhood, my own in particular.'

Not all the truth. Part of her interest was retaliation against Felix's attempted gaslighting. Proving through art that she was worthy. Potent. Special. More than a match for him.

Felix had hated those paintings. By that point, Scarlett suspected he'd even begun to hate her. Certainly, he'd loathed her burgeoning creativity and success. It had made his own artistic failure more acute.

'Can I see them?'

'No.' The reply came out sharper than she'd intended.

'Oh.' Sam's next words were careful. 'You sold them?'

'No. One I gave to my friend. The other I gave to my mum.'

'And the other?'

'Destroyed in a fire.'

His eyes widened. 'A fire? At your house?'

'Something like that.' Scarlett dumped her barely sipped tea. 'We should get back to work.'

'Sure.' Sam guzzled the remainder of his water, watching her the entire time. She could feel his curiosity like a vibration. He wanted to ask and for some reason she wanted to tell.

Scarlett marched back to her easel. Recalling that night

would risk tears, and she would not cry. She would not. Not in front of Sam, and definitely not over Felix.

The turd didn't deserve her precious tears.

TWELVE

SAM GLANCED at Scarlett as he pulled into the carpark at the rear of the restaurant. Her hands were knotted together in her lap, her pink doll's mouth thin. Despite her pensiveness, she looked beautiful. The green of her dress matched eyes made smoky and dark with makeup, and she'd styled her hair into a fancy braid that ended in a knot at the base of her neck, exposing the creamy skin of her throat.

He reached across to briefly squeeze her hands. 'Nothing to fear.'

Her glossy lips parted. 'What makes you think I'm scared?'

Sam finished backing into a space before answering. 'Body language.'

'I'm not scared.'

He raised an eyebrow.

Scarlett sighed and undid her seatbelt. 'Not for me. For you.'

'Me?' He huffed out a laugh. 'I'll be fine.' Sam leaned close, his smile teasing. She smelled deliciously like vanilla ice-cream and looked just as lickable. 'I'm a well-brought-up boy. I know how to behave in a restaurant.'

'I'm sure you do.'

'So, why worry?'

She glanced at the restaurant's kitchen door as though fearing what might come out of it. 'Do you know Audrey Wallace?'

'Not personally. Mum does, I'm sure. Why?'

Scarlett sucked on her bottom lip. Sam wished he could suck on it, too. 'She's likely to take an interest in you.' She regarded him from under lowered brows. 'A deep interest.'

'Okay,' he said, although he wasn't quite sure what Scarlett was getting at. 'This would be a bad thing? From what I understand, having a Wallace take an interest in you is a positive. You never know,' he patted his shirt where his embroidered business logo sat over his chest, 'tonight could be the making of Sam's Dairy.'

'Her interest might not be ... for business purposes.'

'Not for business purposes?'

'It might be ...' She breathed in. 'Sexual.'

Sam spluttered a laugh. Audrey Wallace was rich, privileged, involved in every Levenham event going and considered a local treasure. She was also in her eighties. Sam was an easygoing, open-minded guy, but a woman as old as his grandmother? Not even as a joke would he be going there.

He clocked Scarlett's face and his laugh dissolved. 'Bloody hell, you're serious.'

'Completely. Audrey likes attractive young men. A lot. And she can be particularly aggressive when she's had a few, which is most of the time.'

'Right,' said Sam, rubbing the back of his neck. Then he grinned. 'Don't worry. I'll fight her off.' He indicated the restaurant. 'Come on. Kai's a gun cook and I don't want to miss any of the food.'

Monday nights in Levenham were typically dead, but tonight the street opposite Civic Park was busy with people heading to the front entrance of Restaurant Ten. Kai himself was manning the door, welcoming guests in his usual demonstrative manner.

Spotting Sam, the big chef fairly crowed with delight. He enveloped Sam in a man hug, pounding his back with a broad fist. 'Sam, my main milk man!'

Sam returned the hug and thump, and pushed Kai away before he got whomped to death. Grabbing Scarlett's hand, Sam pulled her close. 'This is my plus-one, Scarlett Ash.'

'*Ma cherie!*' Kai trilled in a bad French accent before wrapping Scarlett in a hug, too. '*Bon soir! Merveilleuse* to see you again.'

Sam gave her a curious look.

Kai answered his unspoken question in his normal Aussie drawl. 'Scarlett sometimes lunches with Audrey Wallace.' He waggled a finger and tutted. 'Not for a few weeks, though.'

'I've been busy.'

'Ah, working hard on your art.' Kai bent close, his voice low. 'Have you given more consideration to my proposal?'

'I have and I honestly can't fit it in.' She patted the big man's shoulder. 'Sorry.'

'A shame. A nude of me on the wall would have brought in the crowds.' Kai looked up and broke out into an enormous grin. Turning from them, he spread his arms wide, then, realising he was being rude, he glanced over his shoulder. 'Sorry. Duty calls. Help yourself to champagne and canapes. I'll catch up later.'

A waitress stepped in front of them holding a tray of

drinks. Scarlett took a glass of champagne while Sam chose a low-alcohol beer.

He pressed his glass to hers in a toast. 'To you, for being my date.'

'This isn't a date, Sam.'

'Okay. My plus-one, then. A very beautiful plus-one.'

'Sam.'

He grinned. There was too much of a smile in her voice for Scarlett to be truly angry. Still, he backed off. 'Yeah, yeah. I know. I'll behave.'

He ushered her through the mill of people, shaking hands and kissing cheeks as he went, and introducing Scarlett. It was hard to keep his satisfaction in check. Sam had always been proud to have Cassie on his arm, but Scarlett made him want to strut like a peacock. She was the sort of woman who turned the heads of both sexes. Yet there was more to her than that. She was smart, intriguing, talented, and her fame, though modest, gave her a sprinkle of glamour the others seemed to want to touch.

Plenty were curious about their relationship. Sam dodged the questions with a joke about Scarlett feeling sorry for him and a change of subject. Kai's food was a welcome distraction, with suppliers eager to humble-brag about their ingredients and talk about ways to grow their businesses.

Sam had just finished discussing veal production with a boutique Red Angus beef breeder, while Scarlett talked to the breeder's slightly awestruck accountant husband about taxation for artists, when Kai's wife, Louise, who was helping as a waitress, presented a tray of tiny tartlets. 'House-smoked trout with mustard and chives.' She pointed to another grouping. 'Local venison-sausage-stuffed mushrooms. And these are kipfler potato rounds with crème fraiche and asparagus.'

'Can I take one of each?' asked Sam.

'Of course.' Louise held out a stack of serviettes with her other hand.

Sam loaded up then flushed slightly when he saw Scarlett's amusement. 'I'm starving.'

'I can see.' She took a stuffed mushroom and popped it into her mouth. Her eyes widened and she pointed to her lips and made a *hurry-up* motion to Sam while she finished chewing. 'That was amazing.' She turned to Louise. 'I'll have to try something else now.'

Sam watched her bite into a potato round, enjoying her pleasure in the food. Scarlett's closed-mouth smile, the shimmer of delight in her eyes as she chewed, was good to see. She was so slim and her cupboards and fridge so lean of produce, he'd wondered if she was one of those permanent dieter types.

'Good to see you eating.'

'Why? Do you think I'm one of those special beings who live on air?'

'Special being, yes. Live on air, no. You have to admit your fridge is pretty barren.'

'I know. I've been terrible at looking after myself lately. Too distracted.'

'I'm definitely going to have to treat you to some Port Andrews takeaway.'

Scarlett sighed. 'And there I was thinking you were a candlelit-restaurant kind of man.'

Sam's response was curtailed by the arrival of Nick Burroughs, a hay producer from nearby Mount Pitt whom Sam knew from his football-playing days, and Nick's girl-friend, Chrissy James, who was making a splash as tourism officer for the Levenham and District Grapegrowers' and Vignerons' Association.

'Scarlett,' said Chrissy, taking Scarlett's hand and shaking it enthusiastically, when Sam introduced her. 'I'm so thrilled to finally meet you. I've heard so much about you and your work from Audrey Wallace. And you did that marvellous painting for my friend Alice. The one that won her the Show Queen contest. I can't tell you how much that meant to her.'

'Thanks,' said Scarlett stiffly.

Sam glanced at her. He had two sisters and recognised the rise of female hackles when he saw them. Which was weird, considering Scarlett and Chrissy had just met.

Chrissy didn't seem to notice. 'Congratulations on your residency, too. You must be very excited.'

'Yes, I am.'

Chrissy's beaming smile began to falter as Scarlett didn't say anything further. She glanced at Nick, who took the hint and started asking Sam about his pasture variety choices for the upcoming sowing season. The two men chatted until Nick was interrupted by another producer.

Sam took the opportunity to steer Scarlett aside.

'What was that all about?' he murmured when they were out of earshot.

Scarlett touched her head. 'Nothing.'

'Didn't seem like nothing.'

'It's a long story. Something for later.'

At least she hadn't completely fobbed him off and told him to mind his own business. Scarlett didn't strike him as naturally rude. She could be odd but not ill-mannered.

'Ah, at last,' proclaimed a regal voice. 'The model man.'

Scarlett groaned.

Sam turned his head and came face to face with a

heavily made-up elderly lady with crimped silver hair, a pair of pearl earrings that must have given their oysters hernias, and wearing a blue dress made of silky material that draped her skinny body like a shroud. A very expensive-looking shroud.

Audrey Wallace. Sam recognised her from her multiple appearances in local media. He flicked a glance at Scarlett and tried not to laugh at her grim expression.

He held out his hand. 'You must be Mrs Wallace. Sam Greenwood.'

She transferred her empty glass of champagne to her other hand and shook his with a firm grip. Although the pupil of her left eye looked oddly misshapen, both were bright blue and glittered with mischief. 'Please, call me Audrey. Scarlett always has, but she has no respect for her elders. You, on the other hand, appear to have a great deal of respect. Are you a Samuel or a Samson? I do like to address people by their proper names.'

'Neither,' said Sam, bemused. 'I'm a plain three-letter Sam.'

'Oh, I wouldn't call you plain.'

'Audrey,' rumbled Scarlett. Unlike half the population of Levenham, Scarlett wasn't remotely intimidated by Mrs Wallace. If Sam didn't believe it'd upset her further, he would have grinned at her.

Scarlett was something, all right. *His* something. For tonight, at least.

Still gripping Sam's hand, Mrs Wallace addressed her. 'I can see why you've been keeping him to yourself.'

'Haven't you got anyone else to pick on?'

'I have many,' replied Audrey, 'but tonight I choose you.'

'Terrific,' Scarlett muttered, before snagging two more

glasses of champagne off a passing waitress and thrusting one towards Audrey, who was forced to let go of Sam's hand to accept it.

Audrey took a long draught, unashamedly ogling Sam as she drank. 'I understand you have your own dairy company.'

'I do. Sam's Dairy. We specialise in supplying pure Jersey milk. Only small, but I'm still establishing the brand.'

'We? I thought the company was yours.'

Clearly, Audrey Wallace had been checking up on him. Interesting. He wondered whether it was because she was looking out for Scarlett or for herself. 'Sorry, force of habit. Technically I own it, but it's very much a part of Mum and Dad's farm.'

'I understand you're currently supplying to the local restaurant trade and selected food stores. Do you have plans for expansion?'

'I do. But I'm cautious. I want to get myself established first, have systems in place and know that when the time comes to scale up I can do so without too much stress.'

'Prudent thinking.'

'Thanks.'

'Although, taking chances can often lead one to greater heights.' Audrey seemed to address this more to Scarlett than Sam. Her sharp gaze flickered to him. 'I have sampled your milk and enjoyed it very much. Have you considered going into cheesemaking? I understand the law has been relaxed on using raw milk in cheese. It would perhaps show off your unique product better.'

'You've been doing your research.'

She smiled and sipped her drink. 'I always do my research, Sam. And I only back winners.'

He imagined she did. The Wallaces hadn't gained their

massive wealth and influence from investing in or supporting lost causes. 'I have thought of cheesemaking for the reason you say. It's an investment, though.'

'Surely the plant wouldn't be that expensive?'

'It's not the money. It's the time. Time I'd need to invest in learning the processes, the regulations. Time to not only produce a product I'd be proud to put my name to, but market it, too. Time away from surfing.' His gaze met Scarlett's. 'From other things that matter to me.' His focus returned to Audrey. 'No point being a millionaire with no life.'

'Indeed,' said Audrey. She held out her empty champagne flute. 'If you could find me another, Sam, I should be grateful.'

Sam took it and lifted it towards Scarlett in a *want one?* gesture. She shook her head. Sam took a moment to eye them both. Audrey had a fine grey eyebrow raised, as if to ask what was keeping him. Scarlett merely looked resigned.

He plunged into the crowd, grinning.

'How the hell did you get so friendly with Audrey Wallace?' asked Sam when they were driving home. It was nearing eleven, and though he would have stayed all night had Scarlett wanted, Sam was struggling to suppress his yawns.

'She and her daughter, Adrienne, came to a student exhibition at the university. Everyone knew who they were. They're both great patrons of the arts, especially Adrienne. To my surprise, they took an interest in my work. We got chatting and Audrey decided she liked me and invited me out to dinner.'

'Just like that?'

'Just like that.'

'I bet that made the other students jealous.'

'A bit.' Her voice quietened. 'Some more than others.'

He glanced across, but Scarlett had turned her face to the window. Moonlight and starshine rimmed her jaw in silver, enhancing her angelic complexion.

'Adrienne had something else on that night,' said Scarlett, her voice returned to normal, 'so it turned out just Audrey, Charles Markham, an old journalist friend of hers, and me. They took me to a restaurant in town and drank me under the table. Thank God I wasn't paying the bill. It must have been horrendous.'

'I imagine someone like Audrey would have very expensive tastes.'

'She does and is completely unashamed about it.'

Sam chuckled. 'I doubt anything shames her. So you kept in touch afterwards?'

'Pretty much. We'd often meet when she came to Adelaide, which was fairly regularly. Audrey has glaucoma and sees a specialist there, and she likes to poke her nose in at galleries and auction houses to see what's happening. I enjoy her company. She never minces words and is a lot of fun. She's been good for my career, too, introducing me to people, offering business advice. And after the fire—' She inhaled sharply and her gaze returned to the side window and the starry night behind.

'Scarlett?'

'Yes, sorry.' She cleared her throat. 'After the fire, she suggested I move to Levenham. I was eager to get away and it seemed a reasonable choice at the time.'

Whatever this fire entailed, it was painful.

Aware he was treading on sensitive territory, Sam kept his tone casual. 'A big move.'

'Yes.'

'And a good one?'

'It was until my creativity decided to go on permanent holiday.'

Although Scarlett's tone was wry, Sam curled his fingers tight around the wheel to stop from reaching for her. 'It'll come back.'

'I hope so.'

He indicated and turned down Scarlett's road. In a few minutes the night would be over, and Sam had no idea when he'd get another chance at this degree of intimacy. Despite her protest otherwise, the evening had felt like a date. They'd had fun, shared laughs, stood close. They'd acted like a couple, or, at least, close friends on the edge of becoming something more.

'This fire,' he said. 'Can I ask what happened?'

Scarlett didn't reply. The headlights caught the entrance to her driveway. Sam twisted his hands on the wheel. He slowed, jaw clenching as he indicated, wanting to smack himself in the head. Scarlett was staring straight ahead, her lips pressed together and a furrow between her brows.

He braked in front of her house. A cat stared at them before trotting off into the night. The lights cast bright circles on the windows.

'Sorry. I shouldn't have asked.'

Scarlett unclipped her seatbelt, but instead of opening the door, she edged onto her hip to face him. Her gaze skipped over his face as if checking for something, then she breathed out and leaned her head against the headrest.

'Felix happened.'

THIRTEEN

'ONE NIGHT ...' The words came on a choked breath. The painful scratch in her throat making Scarlett wish she hadn't started. But this was Sam. Kind, sweet Sam. She cleared her throat of the pain and went on. 'One night, when I was out with Audrey and Charles, Felix collected up all my works—my paintings, sketches, notebooks—and built a pyre in the backyard. He waited until I came home...' She swallowed. 'Until I stepped outside and saw the pyre. My efforts, my dreams, made fragile. Stripped of their power. Power he now held. When he saw I understood that transfer, the horror of it, he set the pyre alight.' She turned her stinging eyes to Sam's. 'He'd doused it with kerosene. Combined with the paper and oils in the canvases, they went up like fireworks.'

'Jesus Christ.' Sam's anger flared like heat. 'Why the hell would he do that?'

'Mental illness.' She smiled sadly. 'Brought on by the failure of his dreams and made worse by substance abuse.'

Sam shook his head, as if that was no excuse. It was,

though it had taken Scarlett a lot of soul-searching to accept. 'I can't imagine the pain of what you went through. Seeing your work destroyed.'

'It wasn't just the work. It was the destruction of us, too,' she said, her gaze unfocused as she remembered. 'Things hadn't been good for a long time, but I kept hoping we'd make it somehow. That night ruined any chance of that. I knew that I had to get out. It was too dangerous.' Because if Felix could coldly destroy her heart's work, how small a step would it take before he turned on Scarlett?

'That's when you came here?'

'Not straightaway. I went to Mum's for a while. That was never going to last, though. We're both too independent, too covetous of our space, and with all the stress, I wasn't great company, either.' She sighed. 'Felix and I had been a couple since university. We'd made a life together. There was so much mess to tidy up. The house. Our possessions. Investments.'

'I guess that's where my mum came in.'

'Yes.' Scarlett smiled at the mention of Karen Patzel. 'She was a godsend. So was Audrey for introducing me to her.' Both strong women, and the perfect people to help her reclaim her own strength.

Sam reached for her hand. Scarlett let him take it. 'I'm glad you had them.'

'Me too.'

Her fingers curled against his. She shouldn't be doing this, but his touch was irresistible. Sam made her feel safe. Safe and understood and cared for. 'I used to have moments where I blamed myself.'

'Why would you do that?'

'I don't know. Because it was my rise that made him fall

so far?' At Sam's puzzlement, she endeavoured to explain. 'Felix was an artist, too. A sculptor, although he experimented with a lot of different media and styles. We all believed that he'd go far.' She pressed her free hand against her chest. 'I certainly did and was one of his biggest supporters. His greatest champion. Felix's work could be fascinating, when he put his mind to it. We were considered a golden couple, destined to fire off one another, like blazing comets. Each other's muses. Except Felix never lived up to his potential. I don't know why. Perhaps he was becoming ill even that early on. The more success I had, the more his jealousy grew and the more it rotted his talent.'

'And the more he blamed you.'

'Yes.'

Sam was silent and Scarlett could see from the thin bent of his mouth his struggle to understand. She couldn't blame him. In Sam's world, such actions would be unthinkable.

'He lost his dream,' she said. 'And in his rage and despair, he tried to ruin mine.'

Sam's fingers folded closer around hers. 'But you're made of tougher stuff.'

'I am.' She looked towards the dairy. 'Or I used to be. Given the way things are right now, I'm not so sure anymore.'

'I am.' He lifted her hand and gave it a jiggle. 'You're brilliant, Scarlett Ash.'

'And you know this how, Sam Greenwood?'

He leaned so close she could feel the caress of his breath on her lips. The golden flecks in his eyes were dancing like fireflies. The urge to turn that caress of air into a touch of mouths was enormous. 'Don't you know? I'm the perfect man.'

Scarlett laughed and tugged her hand from his before

she did something stupid. She opened the door and smiled at him over her shoulder. 'Thanks for tonight. It was lovely.'

'Anytime.'

Her legs didn't want to move. Scarlett made them. The air was cool and scented with grass and irrigation water. She breathed it in, using its freshness to clear her head and heart of all the Sam feelings colliding there. Then with a last wave, she closed the car door.

'Scarlett?'

Sam's window was down, his arm dangling over the edge, his forefinger tapping the duco in a nervous twitch.

'What?'

'We could do more stuff like tonight. When you come back from London.'

'Oh, Sam.'

At first he didn't get it, then his beautiful hazel eyes, so twinkly in the car, dimmed. 'You're not coming back to Levenham.'

'No. It wasn't ...' She swallowed. 'It wasn't my plan.'

He nodded and she could see him trying to gather himself. He gave her a strained smile. 'I'll see you on Wednesday.'

'I look forward to it.'

Scarlett remained on the concrete apron until his tail-lights dissolved into the inky night. It was late, she should go inside, yet sadness held her anchored.

She stared up into the heavens. This far south, uncontaminated by city lights, the Milky Way cast a veil of brilliance across the sky. Its glow left lacey designs on her skin. She studied the patterns, committing them to memory, and as the minutes passed so faded the anguish from Sam's hurt. In its place came a strange, rising hope.

Scarlett held out her palm. Silvery light tickled the

mounds and hollows, beautiful and magical. Awe crept up her spine and shuddered across her shoulders, as though she'd been touched by a god.

'Oh.' The word stretched along her quivery breath.

Heartbeat rising, Scarlett tilted her face once more and beamed her smile back to the stars. She inhaled three deep breaths, drawing her growing inspiration deep inside, trapping it close. Scarlett was no Van Gogh, but this moment, this marvel, made her wonder if this might be a little of what he felt when he saw the morning star from his room in Saint-Paul asylum, and went on to compose *The Starry Night*.

'Thank you,' she whispered. Then she whirled and ran inside to her easel.

The day was blustery, the sea grey and choppy. The sun shone most of the time, when not blocked by scudding clouds, enough to keep the temperature above cold. Just. Not ideal conditions, but nothing less than a freezing storm could have ruined Scarlett's high.

Or her demanding, tumultuous need.

Sam gazed over his shoulder at the messy waves breaking in a gully between two reefs and looked back. 'You sure we have to do this today? The surf's terrible.'

Scarlett hesitated. The gully seemed narrow to her, the reef edges jagged, and apart from a shallow sandy beach and a few rockpools, the cove was surrounded by sharp outcrops that had once been ledges in an ancient seabed. The Shark Hole hadn't been her choice, it was Sam's. Scarlett didn't have enough knowledge of the coastline to locate a site that was both isolated and suited her artistic vision.

As for the name, Sam had assured her when he'd suggested the site that it was a nickname. The sharks in question were wobbegongs, a kind of carpet shark, and relatively harmless unless hassled.

Still, need or not, Scarlett worried for him. 'Are you sure it's safe?'

Sam grinned. 'Yeah. It just looks dangerous. I know what I'm doing.' He glanced at the ocean again, his mouth twisted up in one corner. 'I can't promise anything pretty, though.'

'I don't want pretty. I want you.'

His mouth twisted even further, except this time downwards, and Scarlett could have kicked herself for her poor choice of words.

'I didn't—'

'I know you didn't,' he interrupted as he hoisted his surfboard higher under his arm and slung her one of his easy Sam smiles. 'Guess I'd better get on with it.'

She touched his forearm lightly. 'Thank you. I know you have more important things to do.'

He caught her hand and squeezed it. 'Nothing that can't wait. Besides, I love surfing.'

Scarlett watched him jog lightly towards the sea, mesmerised as she always was by his beautiful shoulders, her stomach still tight and her heart still fluttery from his touch. From emotional longing for more than what they could have, and a hunger to bind Sam to her forever. He was *hers*. An inspiration gifted to her on a warm starlit sky by some unknown force, triggering a frenzy of creativity that had, until a few hours ago, bordered on madness.

But what an incredible, breathless, exhilarating madness it was.

In the scant two days since she'd seen him, Scarlett had

done little else other than work. The frenzy had left the apartment and, to a lesser extent, herself, in chaos. Torn-off charcoal drawings and exploratory paintings were scattered around the old dairy like oversized confetti. Half-drunk cups of tea sat cold and scummy on various surfaces, one with a brush absent-mindedly dunked inside. She'd worked at the easel, on hands and knees on the floor. Standing up, sitting down. At one point, she'd dozed off, her cheek in a puddle of colour she'd been mixing. Woken by Jed's herd, lowing as they ambled to milking, Scarlett had blinked before unthinkingly scraping her cheeks and her hair back, smearing sticky paint further over her face and into her hair.

That morning, as the Wednesday dawn had bled apricot and indigo into the horizon, she'd stood in the centre of the room with her hands on her hips and surveyed the beautiful disaster. By then she'd worked out what she needed: Sam. Not Sam posing unnaturally in front of her, but Sam being Sam. Happy, free Sam.

Her starlight-gifted muse.

He'd greeted her request with bemusement in his voice and a warning that his mate Dylan's morning surf report hadn't been great. Scarlett didn't care. It wasn't the surfing that mattered. It was Sam being in his element.

It was only after she'd hung up that Scarlett had realised she hadn't showered since late Monday afternoon. The layered-on sweat, dust and paint proved difficult to remove, and she'd had to wash her hair twice to get the paint out.

In deference to the wind, she'd bound it in a thick plait that was now hidden by a broad-brimmed hat. A long-sleeved cotton shirt protected her arms and she wore her usual cargo pants to cover her pale legs. Only her feet were bare.

Sand grains squeaked against her feet as Scarlett carried her camera bag closer to the tide mark and set up her tripod. Sam was almost to the reef tips, the muscles of his back flexing beneath his skin-tight gunmetal-grey wetsuit as he guided his board towards the waves.

He waited, bobbing, as she mounted the camera and adjusted its lens. Though not her first love, Scarlett appreciated the merits of photography and was well trained in the art's technical aspects. Her equipment was of high quality. Handy for when she wanted to make digital prints, as she'd done for Alice Lindner with the cursed *Crowns*.

She waved to Sam, who waved back and immediately paddled into the path of a swelling wave.

A half-hour passed before Sam began to propel his board to shore. Scarlett was restless with dissatisfaction. Again, something was missing and again she couldn't grasp what. The photos were good, some of them even beautiful as the closing-out waves drew Sam close to the bottom of the reef and his body became silhouetted against its darker, menacing shade. They would not be wasted, acting as references to the idea that had formed overnight but had yet to reach full fruition. And she had better faith now that it would. What she'd captured today would provide something to work with until she did.

She sighed and gave up scrolling through the images. If there was one thing she'd learned since her mojo had disappeared, it was that neither force nor sulking would bring it back. She stepped from the camera and looked up.

The breath snatched from her chest.

Sam was wading through the hip-deep water, one hand on his floating board, the other trailing fingers in the surrounding light foam. The clouds had spun away, spotlighting him with beams of bright sunshine. Water sluiced from his body, the remaining droplets glinting like crystals. Sam's curls, heavy with moisture, fell in tangles to shoulders made even broader from exertion.

He was grinning widely, like he'd had the best fun of his life.

'Oh my God,' Scarlett whispered. And her awe wasn't all because she'd found her perfect image. It was the heart-stuttering excitement of attraction turning wild.

He was still grinning when he arrived in front of her. 'How'd I go?'

'Perfect.' Then she laughed and grabbed his face between her hands and kissed him on the mouth. 'Absolutely perfect.'

'That good?' he asked, sounding slightly dazed.

'That good.' She put her forefinger to her bottom lip. 'I was wondering though ...'

'Yeah?'

Sam's gaze was locked on her mouth and for a moment Scarlett forgot what she wanted. She dropped her hand. *Focus.* She had to focus before her creative vision disappeared. Or she wrestled him to the beach and kissed him stupid. 'Could you come out of the water again?'

'Sure.'

'Without your board.'

Sam shrugged. 'No problem.'

Scarlett paused, frowning slightly as she considered. If Sam wouldn't be surfing, then he wouldn't need the wetsuit. Or anything else.

She checked either side of the cove. The rocky outcrops were empty. Sam had said it would be like this. The Shark Hole tended to be a local surfer's haunt and then only when the waves were right, which today they weren't, and tourists preferred the steeper cliff of the Port Andrews lighthouse promontory to catch ocean views.

'That's great. Just one more thing.'

'For you? Anything.'

'Would you mind doing it naked?'

SAM PAUSED at the old dairy's flyscreen door and rubbed his chin. Scarlett was on the floor, crouched over a canvas, tongue slipped between her lips as she drew a line across the surface. Her laptop sat alongside, a nude photo on the screen of Sam wading out of the waves at the Shark Hole, while house music doof-doofed from a small portable speaker.

He'd been bursting to see her again since the beach. There'd been no respite from his longing. If Sam wasn't dreaming about her—usually disturbing, highly erotic dreams, sometimes involving rampant greenery like in her paintings—he was wandering the farm in a lovesick daze, mooning like a calf over the soppy daydreams that kept playing out in his brain. His dad kept looking at him and shaking his head. His mum had regarded him with pity, which Sam supposed was reasonable, given the circumstances, even if it was embarrassing.

Delayed past lunchtime by yet another drama with his bottling plant, he'd driven like an idiot to get here, to find

Scarlett so caught up she hadn't noticed his arrival. Most likely, she'd forgotten it was his modelling day.

Rejection bore down on his shoulders like a lead cloak. He'd known from the start that their relationship was about her art, not him, yet that hadn't stopped him from hoping. Even the revelation that she wasn't planning to return to Levenham had set him back only temporarily. There was no reason he could see why she couldn't come back. She was an artist, her work was portable. She liked it here.

She liked *him*. Sam wasn't blind or inexperienced. He recognised attraction when he saw it. Chemistry had swirled between them from their first meeting and grown stronger as their friendship had deepened. Monday night in the car, not only had she shared something personal and painful, she'd been a breath away from kissing him.

Sam understood why she might be afraid of starting something. Scarlett was about to embark on the opportunity of a lifetime, and a romantic entanglement would be more than inconvenient. For a sensitive artist already suffering a crisis, it could even be damaging.

So could not following your heart.

Which is why he'd decided his job now was to make her want to return. A task that would be a hell of lot easier if she would actually pay attention to him.

He rapped again on the doorframe, this time harder. Scarlett glanced up, annoyance creasing her brow, then she realised it was him and smiled in a way that bounced his heart around his ribs and made his blood turn hot.

'Sam, I'm sorry. I didn't hear you arrive. Come in.'

He pushed inside. 'You were deep in concentration.'

She sat back on her haunches and regarded the canvas. 'I was.'

He scanned the room as he crossed to her. The blinds were tilted fully open, flooding the space with light and exposing the shambles it had become. Papers scattered the floor. Some held down with a cup or water glass, others with a pencil or stick of charcoal discarded on top. A few of her canvases had been extracted from their piles and placed around her easel—he guessed for reference—on which a brightly coloured half-completed painting sat. The drawers of her trolley were open. Next to one of its castor wheels, a lidless paint tube had fallen, colour coughing from its mouth like a blue-tongued lizard.

A packet of spicy fruit-roll biscuits lay open on the kitchen bench, along with—horror of horrors—a bottle of his milk. The bedroom zone was just as bad. Her doona lay in a messy lump on her bed, partially covered by the bottom fitted sheet that had sprung from one corner. A wet towel lay on the floor outside the bathroom door, a pair of red knickers alongside.

Scarlett herself wasn't much tidier. Her khaki cargo pants were stained with charcoal and paint splotches, her snug singlet the same. She was barefooted and, he couldn't help noticing, bra-less.

'I guess this means you've had a breakthrough,' he said, trying to sound nonchalant and his gaze averted from the nipple buds peeking through her top.

'I have.' She beamed at him, green eyes glittering like emeralds. 'And it's all thanks to you.'

He laughed, although he didn't really feel that amused. Apart from those brain-frying nipples, Scarlett looked a bit too manic for his liking. As for the state of the room, he'd never seen it like this. It made his nerves jangle.

Sam headed for the bench and the hopefully unspoiled milk. 'All I did was get my gear off.'

Which had been far from the sexy fun he'd imagined it

would be. The water temperature was fifteen degrees and made to feel worse by wind chill, and not conducive to presenting his manhood at its best. Scarlett had made him come in and out of the water about a hundred times, while she either stood behind her camera or skittered back and forth along the shoreline, snapping him from every angle imaginable.

Sam had been cold and fed up by the end of it, but Scarlett had been ecstatic, bouncing around with girlish glee, then kissing him smack on the mouth before bolting to her car and revving off like a hoon.

He felt the plastic of the milk bottle, opened the lid and gave it a sniff, and shoved it into the fridge. He grimaced at the interior, bare except for some floppy celery and a half-filled bowl of what looked like tomato soup. Christ.

Sam closed the fridge door and regarded her. Scarlett was eyeing him back, her head tilted, cupid's bow mouth pursed.

'What?' he said.

'Just thinking.'

'About what?'

The frown returned. She shifted her focus to the computer screen, then to her canvas. She tapped her pencil against her fist and looked at him again.

Finally, she smiled. 'Can you undress?'

Life-models, Sam decided, were worth a bucketload more than the piddling going rate he was being paid.

They were nearing the end of their time, and Sam was stiff and bored and worried. Scarlett had been working like a maniac. Not only sketching, but painting and photographing. She flitted from one project to another, swapping her sketchpad for a canvas, discarding that in favour of her camera, then fiddling on her computer. She was like a child overwhelmed with her Christmas presents.

On the few occasions he'd tried to make conversation, she'd either answered in monosyllables, asked him to keep it for later, or had been too absorbed to notice he'd spoken.

He was standing in front of her naked. Naked and close. No lapping water around his hips offering cover. Just him and his jewels on display, body in a half-twisted crouch, like a seedling corkscrewing its way through soil to the sun. 'Being born,' was how Scarlett had put it. He hoped that didn't mean she thought him baby-sized, although after Wednesday's shrunken efforts, anything was possible.

Sam let out a soft sigh. Here he was on full display and the woman he was mad for could barely register his masculinity. Worse, he couldn't console himself by perving at her nipples in case it set his cock off.

'I heard that,' she said, a smile in her voice.

It took a second or two before Sam realised she was referring to the sigh and not his thoughts. 'Sorry.'

She slid him a look and this time it wasn't one of her frowning glances or absorbed studies. This time it was pouty-mouthed and cheeky. Sam's groin stirred. As if sensing it, Scarlett's focus edged lower. Her lips twitched slightly before she lifted her chin and reconcentrated on her sketch.

Huh. Maybe she did register him.

Minutes passed. Sam fixated on working through financials in his brain. Thinking about the bottling plant had to be better than thinking about that look. He was uncomfortable enough without adding a hard-on to the equation.

'I am impressed, you know.'

Sam blinked. 'Pardon?'

Scarlett tipped her head, indicating his groin. Suppressed laughter was making her mouth twitch. If her eyes were emeralds, they'd be shooting sparks.

'Oh. Right.' Blood rushed to his cheeks, which he supposed was better than rushing southwards. 'Thanks.' Clearing his throat, Sam pulled himself together. 'Good to hear.'

Her expression turned serious. She set her hands in her lap and swivelled her stool to face him. 'I do understand how you're feeling, you know.'

Sam wasn't sure he liked where this was going. Right now, he felt like a jackrabbit in spring. One trapped in a cage while pretty bunnies paraded back and forth outside the bars. 'How's that?'

'You feel like I'm not seeing you. The real you.' She smiled gently and Sam's chagrin gave way to another dose of besotted calf yearning. Christ, she was special. 'I've worked with a lot of models, been one myself. It's easy to feel dehumanised, like you're a statue or a piece of meat. You're not. Not to me.' The smile broadened. 'You're gloriously masculine.'

An embarrassing strangled noise escaped out of Sam's throat, and he quickly coughed to cover it.

'It's what all this,' Scarlett swept her arm around the room, 'is about. Masculinity. I'm capturing yours.'

He wanted to tell her she already had it, but his brain had come to a stop. *Gloriously masculine.* Holy shit. The jackrabbit in him was now a mad March hare.

'I'm going to make magic with your image, Sam.'

The urge to ask if she wanted to make magic with him on the floor right this instant tingled on his tongue. He swallowed it back. Instinct told him now wasn't the time. This wasn't about sex. This was arty-farty stuff and it mattered greatly to her.

'I take it you've got your mojo back.'

'More than you can imagine.'

Their gazes locked. Heartbeats passed, Sam's growing faster as the air turned electric with colliding molecules. Chemistry gone as crazy as his March hare.

Scarlett was the first to crack. She slid off her chair and fussed over her work trolley, snatching up tubes and brushes and plonking them down again with no apparent purpose.

'Which means,' she said, head still down, 'that I'm going to have to work like a madwoman for the next two weeks.'

'Two weeks?'

'That's how long I have left. I've booked the removalist for the twenty-third, then I'm off to Adelaide to spend time with Mum before I fly out. I need to make sure I'm properly back on track and ready for London, and the only way to do that is to produce.'

Two weeks. How did time disappear like that? It felt to Sam like they'd met yesterday. Now Scarlett was preparing to leave Levenham, possibly forever, and except for helping her through her block—although what he'd actually done to achieve that was beyond him—and impressing her with his 'assets', Sam had done nothing to make her want to come back.

'Do you need me to pose more?'

'As much as I'd love to say yes, that won't be necessary. Our usual times will be enough, and I have plenty of photographs to work from.'

'You sure? I can, if you need me to.'

'You're sweet, but no. You have work, too.'

He did, but it would still be there in two weeks. She wouldn't.

Scarlett glanced at the microwave clock. 'You'd better get dressed. I can't have you being late for your girls.'

Sam stepped into his trunks, mind working overtime. 'You're low on milk. How about I bring some back after milking?'

'It's fine. I can get some from Jed if I run out.' She laughed at his sour look. 'Yes, Sam, I know it's not *your* milk, but it'll do for a cup of tea.'

'What about food, then?'

Scarlett folded her arms. 'I'm a big girl. I can look after myself.'

Sam deliberately scanned the room and raised an eyebrow at her.

She raised one back. 'So, it's a mess. This is how I get sometimes when inspiration strikes. Sue me.'

'That's my mum's gig, not mine.' He pulled on his jeans. 'I'm not saying you can't take care of yourself.' Although it was clear to him that she wasn't. 'I have to eat too and cooking for one more is no extra work. I can come here after work and whip something up for us both. That way, if you need me to pose or anything, I'll be here. To be honest, I could do with the company.' He shrugged. 'PlayStation with Dylan gets wearing after a while. He cheats.'

'Surely, you do more with your evenings than play computer games?'

Truth was, Sam didn't play games much. These days, Dylan spent most of his time with his girlfriend, Maya, and Sam had books to balance, feed ratios to work on, calving and insemination schedules, herd health, and endless other business and herd monitors to go over. The workload was why he considered surfing time precious. It kept him sane.

He shrugged again. 'I play the guitar sometimes.'

Delight flushed her pale cheeks. 'Really?'

'Not very well.'

'Doesn't matter.' Already her gaze was flitting across her drawings. He could almost see the cogs of her brain working that news in with her image of him.

'Are we on?'

'For what?'

His jaw tightened. This version of Scarlett was hard work. Gorgeous, but an effort. 'Dinner.'

And more.

Scarlett didn't answer for a long time. Sam levered on his shirt, then slowly put on his socks and boots, afraid to match her gaze in case she realised his game. A false hope. Scarlett wasn't dumb. Except maybe her attraction would be enough to get her to play along.

With his clothes sorted, Sam straightened. Scarlett was toying with her bottom lip and staring at her sketchbook. She'd drawn him emerging from the ocean, shoulders surrounded by rolling foam and his hair longer than it actually was and knotted like dreadlocks. Give him a trident and he'd look like actor Jason Momoa in his memorable superhero pose.

Not so bad. Even his mum reckoned Momoa was hot.

'Dairy farmers are good with hygiene,' he said when the silence continued. 'I won't give you food poisoning, if that's what you're worried about.'

That earned him a laugh. 'I'm sure you won't. All right. I don't want you going to any trouble, though.'

'No chance. I don't have time for trouble.'

But he had all the time in the world for her.

FIFTEEN

SCARLETT STOOD BY THE SINK, watching Sam through the shutters and wishing the sick feeling that had engulfed her would fade.

Darling, gorgeous Sam. Her perfect model man.

She let out a low growl. Of all the shitty-bitty-arsed things that could have happened, she had to go and fall in love. Lust would have been fine. A girl had ways of easing that kind of tension. Love, though, there was no easing that. It just grew and grew like a tumour on her heart, feeding on his smiles, his admiration, his touches, his oh-so-sexy glances. Never satisfied. Always hungry for more.

The irony of it made her want to explode in another screechy *Psycho* re-enactment. Her growl morphed into a half-giggle, half-sob. From the approaching lows, Jed's herd was making its way up the lane. It'd be just her luck for him to catch her having another fit.

Sam waved at her from the front seat of his ute, before reversing and turning out of the yard. Scarlett followed the car's progress until it disappeared and then returned to her easel. She touched the face she'd drawn. Serious Sam. A god set to conquer the world.

And her.

Scarlett knew what he was doing with his offer to cook —seduction had glowed on his face like a beacon. For both their sakes, she had to stay strong and not let him succeed. There'd be enough trauma when she left without crystallising their feelings with a kiss or sex, creating expectation when there was none. And she had the disquieting suspicion that this pent-up energy was the fuel for her reignited creativity. What if she doused it?

Best to stay friends. Without benefits.

She bit out a laugh. Friends. This wasn't school. They were adults. With this sizzling attraction hanging over them, friendship was a fool's game.

But it was one she'd have to play.

Sam returned that night with two rib-eye steaks, a packet of pre-washed salad leaves, a bag of frozen chips, two cold beers and a bottle of red wine.

Scarlett regarded his shopping with her hands on her hips. 'What did I say about going to trouble?'

'What?' he said, wide-eyed with feigned innocence. 'This?' He picked up the salad packet. 'Yeah, like scanning that through the checkout was an effort.'

'You know what I mean.'

Sam stuck his fingers in his ears. 'Not listening.'

Scarlett shook her head, but inside she was laughing and from his cheeky grin Sam knew it.

'Here, have a beer.' He cracked the top off one and shoved it at her, then crouched in front of the oven and twisted the control knobs. 'Right. Now for a grill pan.' Not waiting for a response, he began opening cupboards.

Scarlett left him to it. She'd been in the middle of painting when he'd arrived and wanted to get back to work. After a few false starts, she'd finally begun the first serious piece of what she intended to be her masculine series.

Inspired by the David Guetta dance album she'd had playing in the background, Scarlett's thoughts had been roaming around the difference between the two series. Besides their central figures, what would give Sam's pictures the edge she wanted? A particularly guitar-driven song had provided the answer. Where her feminine compositions featured curves and swirls and movement through roundness, this new series would be more angular. The masculine forms composed of sharper, shorter brushstrokes but contrasted against a feminine sea. It was from where life first emerged. The sea god might be a man, but he was birthed by the feminine.

Another frenzy of activity had followed the revelation, occupying her until the light had begun to change and signalling how far the sun had fallen. Not wanting Sam to catch her again with mucky hair, stinky armpits and no bra, Scarlett had bolted to the bathroom for a good scrub.

Which again had made her laugh on exit. She might want him kept at arms-length, yet that didn't stop her from preening.

'Chips are on,' said Sam, wandering over with his beer to stand alongside her. He studied the composition. The sea-god figure was almost complete and she'd moved on to creating the sea. Once finished, its flowing waters would teem with female creatures, some doe-eyed as they admired the god, some wanton, and more than a few baring teeth and hostile gazes. 'This is different from your others.'

'Yes.' She explained her thoughts on the contrasting motifs. 'The artistic core will remain the same, but I think the new techniques will add punch to the theme of emerging masculinity.'

He gave her one of his admiring glances, the one that made her heart open and want to absorb him into her like an amoeba until they were one. 'How do you think of this stuff?'

Scarlett looked away. This longing had to stop. 'Magic? I suppose it's a combination of things. Process and technique. Emotion.' She pressed her thumb and forefinger into her forehead. 'The alignment of the stars.'

'Hey,' he said, touching her shoulder. 'You okay?'

'Fine, fine.' She waved a hand. 'I'm just edgy. I want to get this right.'

'You will. You're brilliant.'

'Sam.' Why did he have to make this so hard?

'Not flirting.' He lifted his palms, but his grin was unrepentant. 'It's the truth. I think you're brilliant. And I ought to know, being the perfect man and all that.'

She laughed, relieved he'd made a joke out of a moment that was in danger of becoming too intimate for safety.

Sam returned to his preparations. Soon, the air was filled with the aroma of baking chips and grilling steaks. Though she should have been working on her sea creatures, Scarlett's brush wouldn't leave her Sam-sea-god alone. It was nice having him here. A glance and she had reference. His shorts and Sam's Dairy polo shirt were no barrier. Her memory was imprinted with his nudity.

From the top of his head to the tips of his toes, Sam was beautiful. Everything about him was well-proportioned, smoothly formed and lovely, especially his manhood. At the beach it had been easy to ignore. She'd been so high on her inspiration and the effort of capturing him to perfection that she hadn't had time to focus on his groin. There was no such distraction at home. Unable to help herself, Scarlett had zoomed in on her photos for a good look. Several good looks that had left her shaky-handed and breathless.

Determined not to prove herself a hopeless perve, this morning she'd remained deliberately aloof. It wasn't until she had sensed his upset and realised that her coldness was a kind of cruelty that she had told Sam how truly lovely she found him.

Naked or dressed.

With a sigh, she added yet another brushstroke to his belly. And another. Much more and her sea god would end up pregnant with layered-on paint.

'Dinner's nearly ready,' called Sam.

Scarlett dunked her brush and wandered over. Sam had laid out the table with placemats, cutlery and wineglasses. A salad bowl that she didn't know was in the cupboard was positioned in the middle.

'Sit,' he said, indicating her chair.

Scarlett took her seat and watched him distribute the chips and the steaks. Then he plucked up the bottle of red, added a splash to the pan and swirled it around.

Carrying the bottle back to the table, he winked at her. 'Mum's trick. Red wine jus. Although Kai would probably call it something else.'

'Whatever it is, I'm impressed.'

'Good. I can't have my "perfect man" reputation being tarnished.'

The steak was delicious, as was the salad and even the chips. Scarlett couldn't remember the last proper meal she'd had. Probably lunch with Audrey. Lately, it had been tinned soup and frozen meals. She liked food, loved to eat and didn't mind cooking. Her art came first, though. Now more than ever.

Something easier said than done with Sam sitting at right angles to her, his strong jaw working as he ate and his hazel eyes glowing with smugness at the success of his meal.

He ignored her plea to leave the dishes, which meant Scarlett would have to help or risk looking lazy or like a total ingrate. Sam chatted about his herd while he washed and rinsed, making Scarlett smile as he shared details of his favourite cows.

'You're a softy,' she said.

'I know. Pathetic, isn't it?'

Scarlett didn't agree. It was nice that he cared so much about his animals. 'I think it's sweet.'

'I think you're sweet,' said Sam. Then his expression dropped. 'Shit. That wasn't meant to be out loud.'

What to say? Scarlett twisted her tea towel as the urge to cry welled up inside her. She wasn't normally a crier, but lack of sleep and the hopelessness of her longing on top of a beer and a glass of wine had left her emotions a mess.

Sam leaned the heels of his palm on the edge of the sink and grimaced. 'Sorry.'

'It's fine.'

They finished the dishes in awkward silence. Scarlett hung up the tea towel and returned to her easel. She stared at her Sam-sea-god, while the real Sam stood in the kitchen with his hands in his pockets and a brooding look on his face as the over-hormoned elephant in the room stomped its heavy foot, demanding an acknowledgement that Scarlett couldn't give.

'Thank you,' she said, then, knowing it was rude but necessary, she picked up a tube of paint and began to mix fresh colour.

Sam hovered. Scarlett concentrated on her palette. Only music eased the silence, techno beats pulsing like the blood surging through her veins. She hated this. Hated being hurtful, but the hurt would only worsen if she lost her strength.

Finally, he got the hint. 'I'll see you tomorrow.'

'You don't have to.'

'I know.'

Their gazes locked and all Scarlett wanted to do was fold herself into his strong arms and succumb to the terrible want tearing her inside out.

Instead, she dabbed her brush in the paint and applied it to the canvas.

'Bye, Scarlett,' he said softly.

'Goodbye, Sam,' she said just as quietly.

SIXTEEN

SAM GLANCED at Scarlett's packed-up life and looked away, swallowing. It was too real now. She was leaving and all he could do was say goodbye and outwardly wish her success while inwardly pleading with her to come back to him.

He'd been existing in a bubble these past few months. A Scarlett-coloured bubble, saturated with rich air, like nothing he'd ever breathed before or ever would again. Now it had burst and all that was left was loss and his intense, foolish feelings.

Feelings the depth of which she didn't know about and now never would.

'What time is the removalist coming in the morning?' he asked.

Scarlett brushed her hair back from her face and grimaced. 'Early.'

'Will you need a hand?' Sam would have to skip milking to provide it, but he'd do anything to delay losing her.

She shook her head. 'He said he'll have staff. Apparently, it's an easy job. The hardest part will be playing jigsaw with the picture cartons so they don't shift in transit.' She straightened from taping a box and plonked her hands on her hips as she regarded the room. For a moment her face was grumpy, then she looked at Sam and smiled. 'Cup of tea?'

'Love one.'

He kept his eyes on her, drinking in as much as he could in the little time he had left. The colour of her hair, the way it curled, silky and soft over her shoulders and back. Her arms, slender but surprisingly strong. The round mounds of her breasts, teasingly shown off by the fit of her long-sleeved t-shirt. Legs he wanted wrapped around his hips. Lips he wanted to kiss until their doll's pout swelled even more.

Sam rubbed his face. This had to stop. The magic bubble was gone. He needed to forget this one-sided affair, learn to walk straight again. Learn to look ahead to a world without her.

He stared at the boxes, eyes wide, swallowing. He couldn't help the feeling that every one of them symbolised failure. He'd done his best to make her want to return— bringing her meals, telling her cow stories to make her laugh, talking about the idyll of his childhood, how growing up as a country boy made him the man he was. Not hiding his admiration of her work, or her.

The previous Sunday, Sam had convinced her to come to Port Andrews for fish and chips on the beach. Afterwards, he'd taken her to his cottage, a stone's throw from the pine-lined esplanade and a five-minute walk to the village's solitary pub.

It wasn't much, but it was his and Sam was proud of it. Scarlett's reaction had made him even prouder. Her eyes had been bright with delight as she inspected the cottage's neat rooms and well-maintained garden, complete with a lush buffalo lawn and surfing, board-shorts-wearing garden gnome and terracotta pots of white impatiens on the porch —presents from his mum and sisters. She'd even commented on how he had room to expand, which immediately had made him contemplate where to best fit an artist's studio. The back corner would be the ideal spot.

That night, his dreams had been full of her and the life they could have. A dream of which he still couldn't let go.

'Sam?' Scarlett's voice was soft, gentle. Her head tilted as she searched his face.

He rubbed his mouth to hide its sad bent. Stupid emotions. Stupid him. Life would go on. There were other women in the world.

None would be her, though.

She touched his arm.

'Sorry.' He forced a smile. 'Miles away.'

'Thinking about your business?'

'Kind of.' He smoothed his fingers over his jaw. He'd showered and shaved at lunchtime in the faint hope that he might get to kiss her. Aware it was another dumb thing. Unable to stop. 'I've decided to buy the bottling plant.'

Funny, but it had just come to him then. He'd been dithering about it, made restless by his feelings for Scarlett, not wanting to commit in case his life changed. But it was changing. She was leaving, with no plans to come back. She'd be discovered or whatever it was that happened to brilliant artists, and her world would expand. Her days in Levenham would become a short line in her biography, something about licking her wounds or finding new inspiration. There'd be no room for him.

Which meant he needed to get on with things, too.

Her face lit up. 'That's great!'

'Yeah.'

Her expression faded at his lacklustre response. 'You're scared.'

He was, but not of the bottling plant. Of the pain that was going to come crashing down on him the moment he drove away from her. 'A bit. It's a big investment.'

'It is, but you'll make it work. I know you will.'

'Thanks.'

The kettle boiled and clicked off. Scarlett squeezed his arm and went through her tea ritual. Leaving the tea to steep, she turned and leaned her back against the bench, hands tucked behind. It made her breasts thrust out. Sam darted his gaze away only to fix on her bed. Unlike the previous fortnight, when she'd been distracted by inspiration, this morning it was neatly made. Another sign.

When he glanced back, Scarlett was looking at him, lips parted, eyes wide and limpid. Goosebumps shivered along his neck and shuddered down his spine. He recognised that look. It was the same one he'd been trying hard to hide.

The air fizzled as their gazes locked. Sam could hear her whispery breaths. His heart was going so crazy he imagined it sounded as loud.

He swallowed. Then wanted to again when her eyes focused on his throat and darted back to his mouth.

'Scarlett ...' His voice was croaky with all the unsaid things.

'I'd better pour this tea before it stews.' She turned quickly, her bottom lip gripped by her top teeth, movements rapid as she spooned sugar into his mug.

'I wish you weren't leaving.'

The spoon dropped, rattling against the mug. 'I have to.'

'I know. I'm going to miss you, that's all.'

She stared into the still-empty mug. 'I'm going to miss you, too.'

'Scarlett?'

She looked at him. Her mouth trembled.

Sam opened an arm.

She came to him without hesitation. He closed his arms around her, holding her firm against his body, his cheek rested on her hair and his eyes closed, smiling against the awful hurt.

'You're going to be a superstar,' he whispered. 'I'm going to be reading about you in the papers and all over the internet. Australia's newest, brightest star, wowing the art world in London and Europe. Frightening the bejesus out of the establishment.'

She gave a soggy laugh. 'The dream, huh?'

'The dream.' He stroked her hair. 'Your dream. And mine for you.'

She made another sound that could have been a laugh or a sob and pulled away. Sam reluctantly let her go.

Scarlett ran fingers beneath her eyes and sniffed. 'This tea's really going to be stewed now.'

'Not stewed, strong.' Like her.

Like he needed to be.

By unspoken agreement they carried the tea outside. Maybe it was because Scarlett didn't want the reminders of packing any more than Sam did. Autumn had arrived at last and the day was cool. Rain a few days before had given the ground a much-needed soak and faint colour was already tinging the landscape as the more aggressive plants responded.

They leaned on a fence and watched Jed's herd. Neither spoke. Everything had been said. What was left had no words.

Tea finished, Scarlett tipped her head back and gazed at the sky. 'That'll be me up there in five days.'

'At least it'll be spring where you're going.'

'An English spring.'

He chuckled then sobered. 'Have you decided on what you'll paint yet?'

'Yes. No.' She shook her head. Her masculine series had gone as quickly as it had come. Eleven paintings, all of Sam. He'd loved them. They were vivid, full of movement, and being a god gave him a hell of a kick. 'I know what I want to paint, but it'll depend on how I feel, I think.'

Sam tipped out the last of his tea. It was cold and bitter and too much of a reminder of how he felt.

'I have something for you,' she said, holding out her hand for him to take.

The move was so natural, so intimate, like that of a couple, it made Sam's heart stutter.

She kept his hand until they were inside. 'Stay here,' she said, letting go and heading towards the bed.

Sam's breath caught.

She opened the wardrobe door and retrieved a canvas. Keeping it face in, she walked back to him, eyes aglow, a smile tipping her mouth. She stopped a few feet away. 'This is for you. My thanks to you for agreeing to model for me. I know it wasn't easy.' She breathed in. 'But mostly, it's for inspiring me. Without you ...' She took another breath, shaking her head and blinking rapidly. 'I owe you so much.'

'You don't owe me anything. I've loved being with you.'

'Me too. And I hope ...' She licked her lips. 'I hope that when you look at this you remember how much you meant —how much you mean—to me.'

Slowly, she turned the painting around.

Sam stared. His eyes flicked from the canvas to Scarlett and back again.

This was no sea god, surrounded by adoring creatures. There were no swirls, no embellishments. Just Sam, bare-chested, jeans low on his hips, his feet bare. He was posed with his hands in his pockets, a lazy smile on his face and his shoulders slightly hunched forward.

It was him. The real him, easygoing and happy. Nothing like the other paintings he'd watched her produce. She must have done it in secret.

He took it from her, gaze tracing the canvas, nerves rattling with awareness.

Blood drained from his face.

She knew.

Sam didn't know whether to be relieved or even more scared. If he mentioned how much he loved her, where would the conversation lead?

Rejection. As it should. There was no turning back now. The boxes were packed. His farewell present was gripped in his hands. It was time to let go.

'It's brilliant,' he said. 'You're brilliant.'

'You think so?'

'Yeah. Yeah, I do. Come here.' Again, he held out his arm for her to fall into.

He cuddled her one-armed, wishing he could do more without risking her precious painting.

'I wanted to capture the feeling of what our time together was like.'

'You have,' he said, kissing her hair and releasing her. He held up the canvas. Better to look at that than at her. 'Thank you.'

'You're welcome, Sam. Very welcome.' She cleared her throat and smiled. 'I guess I'd better get back to it.'

He looked around. There was little remaining to be done and he had work that had been neglected long enough.

Not to mention phone calls to make to the bank and equipment company. 'I suppose I'd better head too.'

They walked outside together.

Sam stopped at the ute and stared at the door. Opening it would make this final and he didn't want it to be final. He wanted her. A promise. A bit of hope.

Suppressing a sigh, he opened the door and placed the painting carefully on the passenger seat. He turned back to her, mouth twisted wryly. 'I guess this is it.'

Scarlett took his hand in both of hers. Her green eyes were liquid and beautiful. 'There's so much I want to say, so much to thank you for.'

'You don't have to thank me any more than you have.'

'I do. I wish I could give you more than my art. I wish ...' She squeezed her eyes shut. 'I'm so grateful to have met you. You healed me.'

'You healed yourself. You always had it in you to do that. I just ... posed.'

'The model man.'

'That's me.'

She sobered. 'Take care, Sam.' She placed her hand on his chest. 'Look after that big heart. It's special.'

He lifted her hand and placed a kiss on her palm, then closed her fingers over it. Then he gave her hands one last squeeze and turned to leave.

In the ute, he wound down the window. She looked as desolate as he felt.

Sam's throat was full of thorns, but he made himself speak. 'Do something for me?'

'What?'

'Keep being brilliant.'

She smiled. 'I'll do my best.'

He kept the smile fixed until she was far out of sight and

Jed's property had faded from the rear-vision mirror, then Sam let out a roar of pain that drew up from deep in his belly and knocked around the inside of the ute. He did it again, his vision blurring.

He pulled over, fists gripping the wheel, panting. He couldn't leave her. He couldn't.

Sam thudded the back of his head against the seat rest. What to do?

He looked at the painting, at the way she'd captured the enchantment in his eyes, the delight in his smile. The happiness of his love.

If Scarlett already knew, what did he have to lose? After all, he had no more of his heart left to break.

His fists twisted the wheel again.

What. To. Do.

Sam checked the road ahead, then the rear-vision mirror. Seconds later he was hitting 'dial' on his phone and spraying the road with gravel in a skidding U-turn.

She was still standing outside on the concrete apron, pale-skinned and tears coating her cheeks. Tears she quickly tried to wipe away. 'Did you forget something?'

'Yeah,' he breathed, cupping her face between his hands. 'This.'

Then he was kissing her and Scarlett was responding and it was if the world had exploded into colour and movement and emotion like one of her paintings.

Their lips never parted as they backed their way inside towards her bed.

'What about milking?' she panted, when Sam laid her down.

'Dad and Malcolm are taking care of it.'

'But ...'

'Shh,' he said, kissing away her protests. 'It's fine. We're going to be fine.'

Not forever, but for one night.

And that would have to be enough.

Sam eased his legs carefully over the edge of the bed and sat up. He looked down to where Scarlett remained sleeping, her hand curled under her chin like a child. Dawn was edging close, bathing her in faint colour, like she'd been gilded.

He wanted to stroke her bare shoulder. Her cheek. He wanted to wake her and tell her that he loved her.

But it was too late for words. They wouldn't last, anyway. They'd be blown away by jet propulsion and ten thousand miles of ocean.

He soaked in the precious moment, then rose and quietly dressed. His memory would be full of this final night with her, when love finally became real between them.

More light appeared. He had to go.

Barely daring to breathe, he leaned across to kiss her cheek. She made a muttery sound and stirred a little. Sam crept out backwards, his focus only on her.

At the door he paused long enough to whisper, 'I love you.'

Then he was gone.

SEVENTEEN

SCARLETT HAD IMAGINED she wouldn't have time to miss Sam, but loneliness and heartbreak had a way of seeping in when she least expected.

Simple things, like admiring paintings in the National Gallery and being sledgehammered by Peter Paul Rubens' pathos-laden depiction of Samson and Delilah. Sipping a ridiculously expensive coffee at a café along the Thames and seeing a couple laughing at one another, their faces illuminated with humour and love. Standing in front of her easel and suddenly being hit by a memory of Sam, hands in his pockets, his hazel eyes sparkly under his curly, surfer-boy fringe.

The pain was sometimes so sharp it reddened her gaze and left her winded.

Today's flash of memory had been particularly bad. She'd been out walking, following the River Lea to where it joined the Thames at Trinity Buoy Wharf, an area populated with cafes and galleries and which vibrated with creativity from its bustling artistic community. Restlessness had seen Scarlett walk more since her arrival in London seven weeks prior than she had since her relationship with Felix began to fail, when she'd found herself leaving the house for hours on end, to escape his sulks and jealousy and to think.

The northern hemisphere spring was almost at an end, the weather growing warmer as summer neared. Yet the day was cool despite the unusually bright sky. Scarlett had been thinking about colour and, as usual, her mind had drifted to the colours of England compared to Australia. A 'green and pleasant land' England was, especially out in the countryside.

A few days before, one of her fellow resident artists—a crinkle-eyed Queenslander who'd been trying to get into her pants from the moment she arrived—had invited her on a trip to the Cotswolds. For inspiration, he claimed, although Scarlett suspected it was more an attempt at seduction.

It had been too opportune to refuse and once Leith had been put in his place—again—she'd enjoyed the trip. They'd picnicked at Bourton-on-the-Water, on the banks of the River Windrush. Leith had poked holes in its extravagant, picture-postcard beauty, complaining about its lack of substance and toughness. Scarlett had simply stretched out and leaned back on her elbows and said, 'I think it's exquisite,' shutting him up.

The colours had reminded her of her feminine series, with its pinks and reds and masses of living, writhing greens, and the pleasure she'd taken in their creation, before *Crowns* had abandoned her in fallow ground.

The Cotswolds' hues had stayed with her, teasing at her conscience, whispering that she needed them. But for what?

She'd been working consistently since she arrived, sketching mostly, and filling the well of her creativity with long chats into the evenings with her fellow residents and ramblings through galleries. There'd been a few lectures, too, organised by the arts group that ran the residency program. Each morning, Scarlett woke with her head swirling with possibilities, and she'd become restless with the need to make those possibilities concrete.

Nothing was forming though. The ideas remained just that, and frustration was beginning to prickle, while beneath it ran the fear of another block.

She'd hoped another walk would help, but as Scarlett arrived at the docklands she caught a glimpse of straggly, sun-kissed hair. The sight arrested her breath and stilted her legs. She stood frozen at the edge of the path, her heart pounding ferociously, as if demanding release from her chest. The shaggy hair bounced as the man moved through the crowd, then he muscled his broad shoulders through a group of people and disappeared.

'Sam,' she whispered, but even as she said it Scarlett knew it wasn't him. The hair lacked the shagginess of a true salt-ravaged surfer's, the shoulders not quite broad enough.

She remained anchored for a long time, annoying people as they were forced to walk around her, muttering under their breath at her selfishness. Scarlett didn't care. Her heart, which had grown so big in her excitement, now felt hollowed out.

Her hand went to her mouth. She pressed her lips, but still a quiet choke came through. She wanted to howl, she wanted to stomp and rage and scream at the people around her.

None of this was their fault. She'd chosen this path. Chosen it long before she'd met Sam and succumbed to his gorgeous smiles and country-boy ease and niceness. She'd known that falling for him would only lead to hurt and still she'd done it.

She stared at the rippling water in despair, all idea of visiting galleries and workshops gone. The colour had been sucked from the day, leaving misery in its grey wake. With a shuddery breath, she turned and followed the path home.

Her hands were still shaking when she returned to the studio. She sat on the bed and stared at them, then at her phone. Perhaps if she heard his voice? She dismissed the thought as it rose. Contact would only add to their pain. They both knew it. It was why Sam had left that morning without a farewell and why she'd feigned sleep when she'd felt him rise and leave. They were done, but both would have the precious memory of that night to cherish.

Minutes passed. Gradually, the shaking subsided. She breathed deeply. What had she learned this year? So much. So very much. That she could be both fragile and strong. That she could love again. That there were good men in the world. That heartbreak was the price of love.

That inspiration came from within and emotion was its fuel. Her job was to draw on it—the beautiful, the ugly, the heartfelt.

Scarlett stood and pursed her lips at the empty space where a canvas should sit. She could do this. If Sam could inspire her once, he could inspire her again.

Smiling, she hauled up a large canvas and set it on her easel, grabbed a pencil and began to draw. An hour later, satisfied with her outline, she began to paint.

She worked into the night. Knocks sounded on her door. Leith calling out that they were heading for The Laughing Devil for a drink and maybe dinner. Too caught up in her world, she didn't answer.

Sometime around three in the morning, exhausted,

paint-smeared and greasy with sweat, Scarlett stood back from the easel, paintbrush in hand, and stared.

A universe of feeling glowed back at her.

A slow smile formed. She'd done it, captured pure feeling in paint. The frightening intensity of love and the heartbreak that ran hand in hand with it.

Two people tripping into the swirling brightness of love.

And over into the bleak grey angles of loss.

She crawled onto her bed, still staring, and fell asleep with the image throbbing behind her eyelids and the knowledge that she'd found her new theme.

When morning came, she began again.

'Are you going to apply?' asked Leith.

They were in the common area, drinking coffee. Leith had pushed towards her a brochure outlining a subsidised residency in Berlin. After four months, he'd given up trying to seduce her—mostly—and settled into the kind of friendship that allowed them to bounce ideas and critique each other's work without fear of offence.

Scarlett pressed her lips together. She wanted to. Berlin would be fascinating, and unlike the London centre it housed artists from all visual fields. Collaboration and communication were encouraged, and it actively promoted exhibitions of its residents' work. Scarlett had participated in a group exhibition only a fortnight before and sold all seven of her works, but beyond a couple of approaches from smaller London galleries, she had no other bookings.

Berlin would also mean extending her stay in London beyond her residency. An extension that would be at her cost. With that and having to fund part of her living expenses in Berlin, she'd either have to sell everything she'd produced so far and probably some of her works in storage in Australia, or dig into her Felix money.

Which somehow seemed fitting. He'd destroyed her work. Why not use his compensation money to expand her creative opportunities?

'Are you going to apply?' she asked Leith.

He shrugged. 'Thought about it.'

She flicked the brochure back his way. 'You should.'

He fingered the edge and regarded the photograph of the building longingly. 'Maybe next year.'

Scarlett frowned at him. 'Are you okay?' Leith might act the laidback Queenslander, but a sensitive artist existed behind that laconic façade. He was young, too, in his mid-twenties—the youngest to have earned this award—and lacked Scarlett's tempered edges. Leith's talent was enormous, though. His thickly impastoed landscapes and portraits were highly expressive, and more than once he'd been compared to Lucian Freud. Unfortunately, his sales were few.

'Yeah. Just ...' He sighed. 'Things are tough at home.'

'I'm sorry.' Leith's family owned a station in Queensland's drought-ravaged southern Darling Downs. There'd been some hope of rain a few weeks before, but nothing had come of it, and forecasts for the coming season weren't positive. Scarlett knew he missed the farm and his family. He'd told her over drinks and it showed in his work, which was becoming bleaker by the day and affecting his commercial appeal.

He waved her off. 'Not your fault.'

'No, but I can still feel for you.'

Leith regarded her with his mouth tilted. 'Such a freaking shame.'

Scarlett shook her head. It was his favourite lament, and one she thought they'd moved past. 'So you keep telling me.'

'Because it's true. We'd be awesome together.'

'No, we wouldn't.' She indicated the brochure. 'Are you sure you can't apply?'

'Not this year. It closes this week and things are too uncertain right now. There'll be other chances.' He held it out and waggled it at her. 'This has your name written all over it.'

It did. Scarlett could feel it. The Berlin residency started three months after London ended, in January, and would run until July. Another six months of being fully immersed in creativity and opportunity and inspiration in one of the edgiest, most exciting cities on the planet.

She fingered the brochure. Berlin, home of Friedrich, Dix, Kirchner, Höch, Pechstein and more. It was tempting, so tempting.

And what did she have to go home to?

Sam's name flashed in her head, igniting a sharp pain in her chest. There was no use pining over him. It had been months now. A man like Sam would have moved on. By any girl's standards he was a catch, but in a small town like Levenham, he was a prince.

She smiled sadly. Model Sam. Perfect Sam. Without him, she wouldn't have found her way back to her art and created her masculine series. Even the loss of him had provided the inspiration for her ongoing series about couples.

Sam understood how much her art mattered. He wouldn't want her to waste her chances. He wanted her to have success, to be as brilliant as he believed and not be content with a half-life. That was the selflessness of his love.

'Mind if I keep this?' she asked Leith.

He grinned. 'I knew you would.' Then he reached across to grab her hand. 'You're good enough. Christ, you're not just good, you're amazing.' His eyes glittered. 'Go for it. Make it happen.' He squeezed, and she felt in that grip the strength of his torn ambition. 'Make great art.'

Later, in her room, Scarlett sat on her bed with her laptop, getting lost in the possibilities that Berlin offered. She inspected the forms, read the fine print, double-checked her eligibility.

She left the bed to inspect her latest creation. Another blazing canvas of an entwined couple, their body radiating reds, oranges and yellows, the throbbing fire of love. In the corners, blues and browns and black tendrils curled in on themselves, like a vortex in waiting. Except for one. It crept, thin, almost smoke-like towards the lovers' toes. A tentacle of heartbreak, searching for an inlet.

The next in the series was already planned. *Parting* would not be an easy artwork to look at. The splitting of souls could never be conventionally beautiful, but Scarlett was determined to infuse it with so much stoic strength it would create its own beauty. The beauty of self-power, of the human prerogative of survival against the deepest emotional wounds.

After that, she didn't know. It would come though. A well of emotion existed inside her, and she'd found the courage to tap into it.

Scarlett blew a kiss at the couple and returned to her bed. An hour later the forms were filled, samples of her works attached.

She hit 'send', her veins flushed with hope.

EIGHTEEN

SCARLETT HUDDLED into her jacket as she crossed Civic Park. A bitter wind skated across the grass and curled around her calves. Her hardy, lace-up boots guarded her feet from the sopping ground, but her thin leggings offered little protection from the gelid air. At least the down jacket she'd bought from Germany was doing its job. Still, she shuddered as a gust shot up its hem to blast her bum.

It hadn't been her intention to return to Levenham. It had been over sixteen months since she'd left, and though time had eased her heartbreak, the thought of bumping into Sam, knowing he would have moved on, found love and happiness elsewhere, was sometimes too painful to bear.

Yet here she was, and as before, Audrey was to blame.

Scarlett had been back in Australia for five weeks. The first three she'd spent with a friend at Berowra Waters, on the Hawkesbury River north of Sydney, but it hadn't worked out. Ruby and her wife, Kaylee, were going through IVF, and despite assuring Scarlett she was welcome, her presence at such an important time felt like an intrusion. And Berowra Waters, for all its rugged beauty, hadn't sung to her. Not like Levenham had done once.

She'd bailed to her mum's in Adelaide, while she worked out what would be best for her career as well as her life. She'd been there less than a week when Audrey announced she would be in Adelaide the following Wednesday for an appointment, and they should do lunch. Alcohol flowed, as it always did when Audrey was involved. Audrey's partner-in-crime, Charles, had joined them and it wasn't long before the pair had ganged up on Scarlett.

'There is no alternative,' announced Audrey in her usual over-enunciated, regal tone, when the topic had moved from Scarlett's overseas experiences to her future. How the older lady kept from slurring after the amount of alcohol she'd drunk was a mystery. 'You must return to Levenham.'

Scarlett suppressed a sigh. 'And your reasoning behind that statement is what?'

'It's where you belong.' Audrey pointed a silver fork at her. 'You produced some of your best work at Jedidiah's.'

'I also suffered the worst creative block in my life there.'

'Which you overcame.' Audrey crinkled her heavily powdered nose. 'Surely you don't wish to stay here? I agree that Adelaide has its advantages,' she tipped her head at Charles, in acknowledgement of his home, 'and is quite a pleasant city, but it is not Levenham.'

Scarlett shared a glance with Charles, who was trying to keep a straight face. Only Audrey could think Levenham was unparalleled. It was a nice town, no question, but it wasn't faultless. Scarlett had liked it, though. A lot.

'My mum's here,' said Scarlett.

'As is that horrid Felix. He's sculpting again, did you know? Dreadful things they are too. Amorphous lumps of bronze sitting on platforms of fake grass. Rather like looking at one of Jedidiah's cow paddocks. Totally meaningless, although the turd reference is quite apt.'

Charles laughed. 'Come now, Audrey, they're not that bad.'

'They are.' She returned her beady gaze to Scarlett. 'Do you really want to cross paths with him again?'

Scarlett didn't. Not because she felt any real ongoing bitterness—too much time had passed for that, and Felix's compensation had given her Berlin. It was the fear that her success might set him back. Scarlett had a name now and an agent actively promoting her work. The Samstag Museum of Art had purchased two of her Couples paintings, and other institutions were making overtures. Being here would be like rubbing it in his face.

But she couldn't stop being who she was because of Felix, either.

'I have a proposal,' said Audrey, when Scarlett hadn't answered.

Scarlett braced herself with a sip of cabernet merlot.

'Rent-free accommodation in the apartment at Camrick.'

Scarlett remembered the apartment in the Wallace family grounds. She'd spent two nights there after the Felix disaster, while waiting to move into Jed's. It was separate from the historic main house, part of the original stable complex. Digby Wallace-Jones had had it fitted out for himself, when he decided living in the main house with his mother and grandmother was too much. It was more than comfortable.

'What's the catch?'

Audrey waved bejewelled fingers. 'No catch.'

Scarlett set her chin on her hand.

'Oh, don't look at me like that.'

'You're forgetting how well I know you, Audrey. There is *always* a catch.'

The older lady huffed.

Charles laughed and wiped his mouth with his napkin. 'She has you there, Audrey.'

'It's not onerous,' Audrey finally conceded.

'I'm sure,' said Scarlett. 'What penance would I have to pay?'

'I can assure you, it would not be a penance.' She set her cutlery together on her plate and took a sip of wine. 'You have, of course, heard of our recently completed renovations to the Levenham Regional Art Gallery?'

Scarlett had, but she wasn't about to concede that she'd been an avid reader of the online version of the *Levenham Leader* during her time away. 'What about it?'

'There is now space to host classes—'

'No,' said Scarlett. 'I don't have the time or the inclination to give lessons.'

'If you would let me finish,' Audrey snapped. 'We have also made studio space available for an artist-in-residence program.'

Scarlett's skin prickled. An artist-in-residence position? That would solve her problems, in the short-term at least.

'I should quite like it to be you.'

Scarlett shook her head to clear it. She needed to think. Artist-in-residence programs were highly sought after for their exposure and income reliability. They also brought responsibilities—workshops, talks, community involvement. Some involved acquisition clauses. It varied, depending on the organisation's objectives.

None were handed out willy-nilly.

'Surely, it's a competitive position? If it's funded, there must be an application process.'

'Of course it's funded.' Audrey lifted her chin. 'By the Wallace Foundation.'

'And you choose who's accepted.'

'Not quite, but I do have a great deal of influence.'

'Naturally,' said Scarlett, suppressing a giggle. 'When does it start?'

'That depends. When can you move to Levenham?'

Which was how Scarlett found herself back in the town she had thought she'd left forever, hurrying across Civic Park and trying to beat the shower of rain threatening the sky above. Where she should have been was in the gallery's studio, but Audrey had demanded she join her for lunch at Restaurant Ten.

'To celebrate your arrival,' Audrey had said. Which was bemusing when Audrey had already hosted a welcome dinner party at Camrick and drinks in the gallery with the other trustees, all of whom seemed to be either Wallaces or somehow in the family's pockets.

Scarlett wasn't thrilled with Audrey's choice of lunch venue. It reminded her of Kai's party and her night with Sam, and thinking of Sam made her sad. Knowing he did his rounds in the late morning, Scarlett had insisted on a one o'clock lunch to avoid him.

It wasn't that she was a coward. She simply wasn't ready. She would be, one day. Just not this day.

The rose garden was denuded of colour. Scarlett grimaced at the pruned bushes and longed for spring when colour would return. When nature would rouse from her winter sleepiness and the air would fill with the scents of potential new life.

Another gust tugged at her coat. She sank her neck into its high collar and hurried on, hands tucked in, head down.

'Scarlett.'

His voice was like being hit with a sledgehammer. Scarlett stopped so fast she wobbled. She kept her eyes closed for a moment, not wanting to look, but she could hear his footsteps on the path as he closed the distance between them. A distance that stretched from Levenham to London to Berlin and back again. Too far for a single man to make on his own.

She sucked in a breath and looked up.

Sam.

Sam with his hands in his pockets and his shoulders hunched and his gaze searching.

'Hello, Scarlett.'

'Sam.'

The pause felt like overstretched rubber. Any moment it would snap, the released energy forcing them together.

Or flinging them apart.

'How are you?' he asked.

'Good. Good.' She wrapped her arms around her middle, wishing this awkwardness away. Wishing her heart would stop thumping with longing and hope, when there was unlikely to be any.

He looked aside and nodded, mouth drawn, as uncomfortable as she was. He looked back at her. 'I read about your appointment in the paper. Congratulations.'

She didn't miss the rawness of his tone or the accusation behind his words. 'Thanks.'

'You're stopping at Audrey's.' It wasn't a question.

'Yes, it comes with the appointment.'

He nodded.

Is that all they were going to do? Talk in short, tight

sentences. Snatch hurried glances. Unsaid things swarming the air between them like hornets, buzzing and dangerous.

'I'm meeting Audrey for lunch,' she said.

'Funny.' His mouth twisted. 'So am I.'

Scarlett's jaw set. Oh, that conniving, meddling old cow.

Sam sighed and rubbed his shaggy hair. Still the same straggly surfer cut, albeit with fewer sun streaks. He was wonderfully, deliciously familiar. She wanted to throw herself at him and bury her face into his chest, breathe him in, revel in his strength. In *him*.

'I guess we'd better get moving.' He half turned, then paused, eyeing her over his shoulder. 'Unless you want me to give it a miss?'

'No.' Her refusal sounded breathy. She cleared her throat and aimed for a stronger, firmer tone. 'No.' Scarlett twitched a smile. 'It'll be good to catch up. It's been a while.'

'Yeah, it has. Fifteen months, three weeks and,' he lifted his gaze to the grey, swirling sky, 'two days.'

She stared at him, huge-eyed. 'You've been counting?'

Sam's gaze locked on hers. 'Every second.'

'Sam.' Heat bloomed behind her eyes. 'Oh, Sam.' Her hand fluttered to her mouth. 'I ...'

He shrugged, his pockets bulging where he'd dug his fists deeply inside. 'It doesn't matter. Counting was just a habit I got into. It doesn't mean anything anymore.'

'Oh.'

Now Scarlett really wanted to cry.

He jerked his chin towards the road. 'We'd better not leave Audrey waiting. You know what she's like.'

They walked side by side to the end of the gardens, waited to cross the road, and stepped out. All in silence. Sam with his shoulders rounded and his hands still deep in his pockets. Scarlett with her neck hunched and her eyes as wide as they could go to dry the tears that kept threatening.

He hated her.

But why? Was it because she hadn't been in touch since her arrival in Levenham? Of course she hadn't contacted him. Why would she want to intrude on his life? They'd shared a brief, intense affair, but that was an age ago.

It doesn't mean anything anymore.

Which said it all. Like her, Sam had felt their parting acutely, and now he'd moved on as she'd expected him to.

She glanced at him. His jaw was flexed, the bones pronounced like steel struts beneath tarpaulin. Tension came off him in electric waves. His eyes fixed ahead. His mouth, though, his lovely, kissable mouth, was curved low.

She swallowed. In the times when yearning weakened the walls she'd built around her heart, Scarlett had fantasised about them meeting again. They'd see one another and happiness would burst like spring buds. There'd be caresses, kisses, murmured words of longing at last fulfilled. Reignited passion.

Love.

The reality was the complete opposite. A nightmare.

They reached the other side of the road. Scarlett stepped up the kerb and stopped, her hand on Sam's arm.

He looked at her and his gaze softened a little. 'You okay?'

She swallowed. 'No.'

'What's up?'

Her chest burned. She flattened her hand over it. Even beneath the layers, her heartbeat pulsed thickly. He seemed so *bitter*. 'We knew this.'

His brow furrowed. 'I don't know what you mean.'

'Us. How fleeting it was. That no matter what we felt, it wouldn't last.'

The corners of his eyes twitched. 'Are you blaming me?'

'Blaming you?' Now it was her turn to be confused. 'For what?'

'For hoping. For counting the days. For thinking maybe we could have been more. For thinking you might have cared beyond the weeks we had. That ...' His voice choked. 'If you did come back here, there'd be a chance for us.'

Her mouth opened. Could this be real?

'You can't blame me for that. Any man would have felt the same. And yeah, it's been a long time and another man might have gotten over it by now, but I haven't, okay? Because I had that hope. I guess I can let go of that now.'

'Why?'

'Come on, Scarlett. It's obvious. You've been back for what? A couple of weeks? And nothing. I had to learn you were back from the frigging newspaper. The only reason we're even having this conversation is because Audrey tricked us into meeting.'

A tear trickled down her cheek. Scarlett swiped at it, angry at the way Sam noticed its fall and the anguish that appeared in his face. She shook her head. 'We're messing this up.'

'Yeah, we are.' He sighed. 'I used to daydream about this moment.' Sam gave an acid laugh. 'It was my "perfect day" dream.' He stared at the street as a car sloshed by. 'Not very perfect.'

'I dreamed of it, too.' So vividly and with so much yearning it had become the centre of her Berlin series, Reunification. A metaphor of the fallen Berlin Wall and love.

His focus jerked back to hers, eyes searching.

She smiled shakily. 'I used to have these romantic fantasies of you sweeping me off my feet and twirling me around, saying my name over and over.'

'Used to?'

She bit her lip. 'I made myself stop. They hurt too much.' Hurt she'd channelled once more into her art.

'Why would that hurt?'

'Because it could never be real.' Scarlett waved a finger, indicating the space between them. 'Point proven.'

Sam stared at her so hard she began to squirm.

'You're a model man, Sam. The perfect man. What was the chance that you wouldn't have moved on by now?'

'What was the chance?' There was no humour in the laugh that escaped him. 'No chance. Not after you.' He grabbed her shoulders, gaze intent on hers. 'Scarlett, you undid me. The only person who was going to put me back together was you.'

Scarlett's mouth opened, closed and opened again. 'There's no one?'

'Only you.'

A taxi pulled up adjacent to them. Scarlett frowned at it, willing her brain to work.

The door opened. Audrey Wallace alighted, her skinny frame bulked out by a voluminous fur coat. After a quick, purse-mouthed glance at Scarlett and Sam, she bent inside the taxi for a last word to the driver, then closed the door and eyed the two of them up and down.

'I see you've found one another. Excellent. Sam, be a gentleman and help me up the kerb.'

Scarlett's eyes narrowed. Audrey needed no help, so what was with the frail-old-lady act?

Audrey regarded them again. 'Shall we venture inside? It's far too chilly to be standing in the cold.'

Scarlett didn't move.

'Scarlett?' Sam's voice was soft.

She looked between Sam and Audrey for a long moment. 'No,' she finally said, digging her nails into her palms. 'No, I don't want to do lunch.'

Sam glanced away, his chest rising as he breathed in deeply. He forced a smile at Audrey. 'Looks like it's just you and me.' He placed his hand on Audrey's elbow and nodded at Scarlett. 'Good to see you again. Take care.'

'No.'

Audrey's finely painted eyebrows lifted.

'We need to talk.' She swallowed, still unsure. 'The two of us. We could go back to the studio, or to my apartment. Or ...' She tried to think of somewhere private. 'The Shark Hole.'

She could see the mirrored want and hope in Sam's gaze, but still he hesitated. 'It'll be cold at the Shark Hole.'

'We could call into Port Andrews on the way for fish and chips to warm us up.'

A slow smile spread like dawn across his gorgeous face. 'We could.'

'It won't be up to Kai's standards, but ...' She spread her arms a little.

'It won't matter.'

'No,' she whispered, her throat feeling thick. 'It won't.'

Nothing would, as long as they were together.

Sam asked Audrey, 'Will you be all right?'

The older lady was as smug as a pug. 'Don't worry about me, I shall be perfectly fine. Ah,' she said, peering past Sam, 'I do believe my luncheon date has arrived. Well,' she regarded them archly now, 'you really didn't believe that I'd enjoy playing gooseberry with you two, did you?'

Scarlett and Sam were too gobsmacked to answer.

'Audrey, a delight as always,' said Barry McClintoff, Levenham's long-serving mayor. He kissed her on both powdery cheeks before beaming at Sam and Scarlett and thrusting out a bottle of sparkling wine. 'This must be for you.'

Sam took it and inspected the label. 'Gratia. Digby's winery.'

'And a very fine drop,' said Audrey. 'Well, what are you both doing standing there?' She made a shooing motion. 'Off you go.'

Sam held out his free hand for Scarlett to take. His grip was warm and firm and perfect.

'You have to agree, Barry,' Scarlett heard Audrey say as they sauntered off, 'that I am a truly inspired matchmaker.'

'That you are, Audrey. That you are.'

Sam threw his head back and laughed. Scarlett broke into giggles.

He smiled down at her. 'Not quite the perfect day.'

'Not quite. But we're getting there.' She leaned into his shoulder. 'Can I tell you something?'

'What?'

'I don't really want fish and chips.'

Sam pressed his lips to her temple in a lingering kiss. 'Neither do I, brilliant girl. Neither do I.'

NINETEEN

SAM LEANED on his elbow and smiled down at the sleepy girl beside him. After so long missing her, of living in a world that felt permanently diminished without her in it, of working his guts out to stop from thinking about her and what could have been, having Scarlett back in his arms felt like a miracle.

He wasn't a fool, though. Scarlett's appointment at the gallery wasn't permanent, and she was a star now, just as he knew she would be. Maybe too much of a star for Levenham.

'I can feel you smiling,' she said, her eyes still closed.

'Can't help it.'

She opened one eye, her lips spreading as she checked out his mouth, then chest. 'I can't help it, either.'

He leaned over to kiss her. 'I like your smile.'

'I like your everything, perfect man.'

He traced a circle on her arm. Her skin puckered with little goosebumps. They never made it to the Shark Hole. And they never made it to the fish and chip shop. Sam had driven to his place, Scarlett following in her car. Her look when she had alighted told him he'd done the right thing.

When they'd finally made it to the kitchen, he'd cupped her face between his palms, checking it for permission, then kissed her. Gently, at first, savouring all he'd missed. Her beautiful, soft mouth, her porcelain skin, her gemstone eyes. Her brilliance.

Gentle hadn't lasted. It was their last night all over again, without the sorrow of her departure dulling the edges of their passion. They'd worked their way to his bedroom, breathless, giggling, turned on, and trailing clothes in their wake.

There'd been no time for talking. Only for touching and feeling and wonder.

Sam swallowed. It would spoil the moment, but he had to know. 'How long are you back for?'

Scarlett's gaze dropped to the doona. 'The artist-in-residence program is for three months.'

'And after that?'

'I haven't worked that out yet.'

'Okay.' It wasn't. Already his heart was aching. He rolled to sit on the side of the bed and stared at the wall, where the painting she'd done of him was hung. When she'd captured his happiness and love.

He knew every millimetre of that picture, had touched every brushstroke. He'd even slept with it, one night after too many beers with Dylan to celebrate his engagement to Maya. It was all he'd had. Her reminder to him of the time they'd spent together, of how much, for a brief moment in time, he'd meant to her.

Not enough, though.

The bed rippled behind him and Scarlett's warm hand pressed against his back. She leaned her chin on his shoulder and pressed her cheek against his. Sam reached for her other hand and squeezed it. It was all right. He'd get over it.

Yeah, right.

'Sam?'

'I should get to the farm.' It was the truth. With the new bottling plant and a contract to supply a local motel as well as the new restaurant clients he'd attracted, he was milking twenty extra cows. He couldn't leave milking to his dad and Malcolm alone.

Except Sam couldn't bring himself to move.

Her finger touched his chin. 'Look at me?'

He turned. Her cupid's bow lips were swollen from his kisses, her eyes limpid. Silken dark hair curled over her shoulders, the ends grazing her breasts. His chest heaved with the urge to cling to her. Damn Audrey for orchestrating their meeting. She should have left them alone. Better to be angry than to have to go through all this hurt again.

'I'd like to stay.'

'No problem. Help yourself to whatever you need. I'll be back around six. There's a casserole in the freezer I can take out, or we can have dinner at the pub, if you like. They do a decent steak.'

'Not *here* here.' She smiled and shook him a little. 'I meant stay in Levenham. Once the program's finished.' Uncertainty made her smile waver. 'If I can.'

'Why couldn't you?'

'I don't know. Maybe I won't be able to find somewhere to live?'

He toyed with her fingers. 'As far as I know, Jed's is still vacant.' He held her gaze, searching for reassurance that her desire to stay had something to do with him. That his burgeoning hope had foundation. 'Or you could move in here, with me. I could shift out all the junk in the spare room for a studio. It won't be very glamorous, but it'd do until we can organise something better.'

Like a proper room in the backyard, the one he'd envisaged all those months ago. A light-filled timber studio, built just for her.

'You're a sweet man.' Scarlett kissed his cheek. 'Why don't we cross that bridge when we come to it? I'm not homeless yet and there's no real rush. Let's enjoy our reunion first.'

She was right. Sam was getting ahead of himself. He couldn't help it. The idea that she might stay made him giddy.

'You might not want me here, anyway. Living with an artist has its challenges.'

'No more than living with a dairy farmer. And let me remind you, I've seen what you get like.'

'Sweaty and smelly?'

'Funny, I remember the no bra more than anything.'

She nudged him. '*Such* a man.'

'A model man, I'll have you know.'

'Yes,' she said, serious now. 'Very model.' She wormed her way onto his lap, draped her arms around his neck and pressed her forehead against his. 'Very model and very perfect. I missed you, Sam. You have no idea how much.'

'If it was anything like how much I missed you, then yeah, I do have an idea. The only way I coped was to work.'

'That's what I did too. Channelled all my feelings into my art.'

He stroked her slim waist. 'The tortured-artist thing?'

'Mmm.' She shivered slightly as he tickled his fingers up her ribs. 'Better than cutting off my ear.'

'Definitely.' He kissed his way from her mouth to her left ear and sucked on the lobe. 'I like your ears.'

'Sam?' He liked her breathlessness, too.

'Yeah, brilliant girl?'

'What about milking?'

'Shit,' he muttered, pulling away and running his fingers over his head. 'Sorry.'

She curled a soft hand around his jaw. 'Don't apologise. You have work to do.' She glanced at the bedside clock. 'And I need to get back to the gallery.'

He removed her hand from his face and kissed her palm. 'Come back here after?'

'Will you shout me fish and chips this time?'

'I can do that. Fish and chips and sparkling wine.'

'And us.'

'Yes,' said Sam, stroking her hair, so full of love he was liable to burst. 'Us.'

'What do you think?' asked Scarlett, holding a dress in front of her naked body. 'Suitable?'

Sam leaned against the door jamb. She was fresh from the shower, her body scrubbed and pink, her just-dried hair styled up in an artistically messy bun, and he was enjoying the view. 'More than suitable. I prefer you naked, though.'

She gave him a look and tossed the dress on the bed, then reached for her underwear. 'This is an important night. I want to look good for you.'

'You always look good.' He entered the room and grabbed her from behind and kissed the back of her neck. She smelled of vanilla. 'Delicious, in fact.'

Scarlett batted him away. 'Sam!'

'What?' His hands were already roving downwards.

'We're late. And you'll crumple your suit.'

'So?' The look she gave him made him release her and raise his palms. 'All right, all right.' He sat on the bed and watched her pull on a pair of silky black knickers. 'It's not that important.'

They were getting ready for the Levenham Chamber of Commerce Business Awards gala at the recently opened Ryan's Vineyard complex. Sam's Dairy was up for the Outstanding Agribusiness award. His nomination courtesy of a certain interfering elderly matron.

A lacy black bra followed the knickers. Sam sighed. How was he meant to maintain decorum knowing that was underneath Scarlett's dress?

'Can you do me a favour?' asked Scarlett when she'd shimmied into a forest-green sheath that clung to her contours and made Sam want to tear it off again. 'Check to see if I locked the studio? I can't remember if I did.'

'Sure.' Anything for a distraction. He had half a hard-on as it was, which was no way to turn up to an awards night with Levenham's good and great.

He sauntered across the back lawn to Scarlett's studio. The floor-to-ceiling glass windows swirled with the colours of the falling sun, like one of her paintings. He'd had the studio built not long after she had moved in five months ago. It wasn't perfect, but it would do until they worked out if they were going to stay in Port Andrews in the long-term.

Scarlett had her eye on a cliff-top block of land on a peninsula not far from the Shark Hole. It was isolated but ideal for her dream of a bigger, more modern house, more suited to a family. Though on a large block, Sam's cottage was small and would take major renovations to bring it to four bedrooms, and at three-quarters of an acre, the Shark

Hole block had more than enough room for a proper studio and a gallery she could open to visitors.

They could afford it, too. With her portrait of Audrey having been hung in this year's prestigious Archibald Prize, Scarlett's sales had exploded. Sam's Dairy wasn't doing too badly, either. So much so his dad was gradually converting his herd to Jerseys to help with demand. Scarlett was even learning to surf—for the negative ions, she claimed, although Sam knew she was doing it for him.

Life was pretty damn good.

'Bloody hell, Scarlett.' He rubbed at his hair, noticing for the first time that the door to the studio was ajar. Port Andrews was a safe little fishing village, but even it had its share of dropkicks, and with Scarlett's works fetching thousands they couldn't be lax about security.

Sam sighed. He'd better check the window locks while he was at it.

The interior was bathed in sepia, giving the walls and workspaces an antique glow and coating the back of the canvas on Scarlett's easel in orange. He was surprised it wasn't covered. She'd been coy about her work lately. Sam had humoured her the way he did all her artistic bents because he loved her. And if she wanted to be secretive, then that was fine by him. Two could play that game.

The thought made his fingers go to his suit pocket and the box tucked inside. He smiled to himself. Later.

Sam checked the windows, glad to find them all locked. Then, unable to help himself, he wandered to the front of the easel.

'Like it?' said Scarlett from the door.

Sam looked at her, shimmering and glorious in her green dress, and back to the painting. All he could do was stare.

His beautiful, brilliant girl had trumped him, and in the most Scarlett of ways. The audacity of it left him wordless.

She came inside to stand next to him, her fingers searching for his.

Sam took them and lifted her hand to his lips. 'This is why you've been so secretive?'

She nodded. 'Do you like it?'

'Love it. And the answer is yes.'

Her smile sent his heart into orbit. 'That's all right, then.'

'Just all right?'

'Okay, it's good. Great.' She wrapped herself against him. 'Fantastic!'

Sam laughed and clutched her to his chest. 'Love you, brilliant girl.'

'And I love you, model man.'

The kiss that followed lasted a long, long time.

'Just to check,' said Sam, drawing away. 'That was a proposal?'

'It was.'

'Good, because ...' He dug into his pocket, amused to find his nerves over the evening had disappeared completely. Scarlett had stolen the show and he didn't mind a scrap. He opened the lid of the box and held it out to her, his heart flip-flopping when her eyes widened and her hands folded prayer-like over her mouth.

'You sneaky man!'

It was a simple ring, white gold with an emerald-cut natural emerald at its centre and two trapezoid-cut diamonds on either side. His mum and sisters had helped him choose it. Apparently, they'd had discussions with Scarlett on the subject of engagement rings and knew what she'd like. That they'd been talking about rings had bemused Sam at the time. Now that he'd seen her painting, he understood how it had arisen.

'Seems like great minds think alike.'

'It's beautiful,' she said breathlessly.

Her hand was trembling when she held it out. Sam caressed her fingers to steady her before sliding the ring on. Even he had to admit it looked stunning.

But everything about Scarlett was stunning.

He glanced again at her painting. A self-portrait in Scarlett's inimitable style—bright and swirly and intricate. She was lying on her side, her face filling most of the canvas, surrounded by flowers and small, bright-eyed peacock-coloured birds. Her eyes were huge and misty green, her skin ivory and shadowed with pale blue, and from her red lips flowed a line of text: 'Be my perfect man forever?'

'Always,' he whispered, then he led her out into the fading sunset. Already the sky was purpling with the approaching night. They were going to be late for the awards, but it didn't matter.

He'd already won.

Rocking
HORSE HILL
CATHRYN
HEIN
A Levenham Love Story

Who do you trust when a stranger threatens to tear your family apart?

When Emily Wallace-Jones's brother Digby arrives home with a secretive new fiancée, no one knows how to react. The Wallace-Jones are old-money rural aristocracy and Felicity Townsend is from a very different side of the tracks.

But Em is determined not to treat Felicity with the same teenage snobbery that tore apart her relationship with her first love, Josh Sinclair. A man who has now sauntered sexily back into Em's life and given her a chance for redemption.

As Felicity settles in, suspicions are raised about her intentions toward Em's beloved Rocking Horse Hill, the historic family property that Digby owns but has promised will be Em's home for as long as she wishes. Though worried for her future, Em sides with her brother and Felicity, until a near tragedy sets in motion a chain of events that will change the family forever.

Discover where the Levenham Love Story series began with this emotional tale of family turmoil and second-chance love.

DEAR READER

Thank you so much for reading *Scarlett and the Model Man*. I hope you enjoyed Scarlett and Sam's journey to love and happiness. If you did, and you have a few moments, I'd be very grateful if you could leave a rating or few words in review to help others discover my books.

If you'd like to know when my next release comes available plus gain access to exclusive content, news and giveaways, please subscribe to my newsletter via my website.

More information about me and my books, including the inspiration behind *Scarlett and the Model Man*, along with plenty of other fun stuff, can be found at cathryn-hein.com.

Web: cathrynhein.com
Facebook: facebook.com/cathrynhein
Twitter: @CathrynHein
Instagram: cathrynheinauthor

www.ingramcontent.com/pod-product-compliance
Lightning Source LLC
Chambersburg PA
CBHW070321120726
47909CB00008B/2543